Culture

By Guy Cook

This is dedicated to my mother, Brenda Cook, who loved stories. I'm sure there's much of her in here.

Acknowledgements

A big thank you to the following people, all of whom have both encouraged me and significantly improved the book:

Andrea Eardley for the painting used on the front cover, commissioned for the book. It shows the west façade of Winchester Cathedral—which you will see features in our tale—interpreted, I believe, to reflect the tone of the story. You can see further examples of her work at www.eardleyart.co.uk.

Nick Thomas at Inck Design for turning Andrea's painting into the actual cover.

My magnificent review team: Betty Chadwick, Carolyn Cook, Stephen Cook, Duncan Eardley, Karl Eldridge, Mike Fowkes, Rob Hodgkinson, Lisa Huckstep, Damien Moore, TW and Ian Wright.

Also, on a technical point of view, to AutoCrit for their excellent online editing software.

Finally, to Winchester, whose modern-day cityscape and rich heritage provide the backdrop to the story.

Chapter 1

Ok, done it. I feel quite sad now—leaving behind the desperate last minute searches for culture, the uncool bands, the weekly blogs, the dubious nature of some of the entries—but I guess that's a sign it was a good thing to do. Of course I can't leave it like that, I need to have changed in some way. I must naturally do the kind of cultural activities I've forced myself to do over the last year. Over and out.

5:00 p.m. on New Year's Eve. Rob leaned back, put his feet on the desk and ceremoniously hit the Enter key to submit his final blog post. A train rumbled in the distance. He stayed still a few moments, before stretching for the mouse and scanning through the year's entries. Settling on one post or another, he lost himself for a while. The satisfaction of a task completed, mixed with a little nostalgia.

Introduction to Rob's Year of Culture

How can I be a cultural icon without any knowledge of culture, you're asking? When I'm not sure I've seen a music gig this decade? When I think a gallery is a type of ship? When my music collection mostly consists of the best of '80s acts such as Tracey Ullman (an excellent album, actually)? Good questions, and here's my response: to indulge in a cultural pastime every week this year.

Week 1 (1-4 Jan): Art galleries of Winchester

My odyssey started on Friday 2 January with the art galleries of Winchester. There were three on my list—one was closed and I couldn't find one, leaving The Minster Gallery on Great Minster Street. I have to confess I like paintings of "real" scenes—landscape, seascape, nature or bustling activity—and struggle with anything too abstract or nondescript (like a plate of fruit). Nothing changed my mind here, but it's only week one. I saw deliberately wrong-shaped people, and over-straight or over-curved scenes; cleverly done, but they didn't really engage me. Where I earned my culture marks, though, was for my appreciation of the Rod Pearce exhibition at the Minster, and my new knowledge of oil paintings. Rod Pearce's paintings portrayed brilliantly atmospheric city and landscapes with water and sky particularly well done. They were mere splodges on canvas, but you could always tell exactly what they were—for example, master and dog in tree-lined twilight lane—without any of the details really being there. I could understand why people would spend two thousand pounds on these. The gallerist told me they were oil paintings (once she realised I didn't know). Culturally enhanced, I headed for a swift pint.

Week 7 (9-15 Feb): Status Quo at Plymouth Pavilions

Need I say more? Friday found me at Plymouth Pavilions for a concert by the Quo—Francis Rossi, Rick Parfitt and all. I sometimes work at my company's office in Plymouth, so I'd emailed to see if anyone wanted to come—all I got was comments about zimmer frames and the search for a fourth chord. Suffice to say, they missed out, not appreciating the sheer superstardom the Quo's longevity and hit-drenched back catalogue has granted them. Like any mega-rock band, the entrance is spectacular—there's a support act, they make you wait and wait, the lights dim, there's an explosion of noise…and there they are, playing Caroline.

The Plymouth venue had a large standing section, which always gives more atmosphere, and easy access to the bar throughout. The concert was high energy, slick, and generally superb, with two hours of hits and a welcome encore. For the record: Status Quo's first top ten hit was in 1968; Rossi and Parfitt have been with the band from the start; they've had over twenty top ten hits and a single number one (Down Down); and, of course, they opened Live Aid with "Rockin' All over the World". Terrific.

Week 37 (7-13 Sept): Running Fox sculpture on St Giles Hill, Winchester

A busy week left me culture-less at 9:00 p.m. on the Sunday (midnight Sunday is my weekly deadline). Which is why I found myself stumbling around a hilltop in the pitch dark, trying to find the Paula Moran seat using the light from my fading bicycle lamp. I had read in the Visit Winchester booklet that "A short walk up to the top of St Giles Hill is rewarded with spectacular views of the city. Rest on the Paula Moran Seat, commissioned in 1995 from blacksmith Richard Bent. Made from hot forged steel, the seat depicts a running fox." There are lots of benches on top of St Giles, most of them with memorial inscriptions—something like an elderly lady who has sat on the bench and loved the view all her life. I anticipated finding something similar, although with no views due to it being a moonless night.

At first, I treated it as a bit of a joke—alone, stumbling in the dark at nine thirty on a Sunday evening, didn't I have better things to do? Then I found the seat after about ten minutes, and, as ever, was engaged. First, reading the memorial, Paula Moran wasn't old, but only thirty-six when she died (in 1994); and second, the seat pointed at the city lights, which did provide mesmerising views. I sat on the bench for five minutes and stared at the lights in what felt a poignant moment, paying respects to someone whose life I didn't know (but her real story does exist somewhere). Thirty-six is far too young, of course.

Rob clicked off the monitor and headed for the shower. He had arranged to meet friends in town at six thirty and was ready in half an hour, favourite shirt untucked and cool. He paused to stare through the window at the dark silhouette of St Catherine's Hill. New Year's aspirations flicked through his mind: his sports injuries needed sorting out once and for all; he hadn't had a girlfriend in ages; onto his perennial ambition, he'd never won a sports tournament in his thirty-seven years; and then, getting a bit carried away, how about learning to fly (which he couldn't afford)…or even, somehow, performing that one act of heroism everyone dreams of. He tapped the window sill, spun towards the door and was gone, en route to a night of pubs, half-remembered conversations and some bad dancing.

Chapter 2

Friday 26 March, noon. Rob sat on the kitchen sideboard and lifted himself onto his hands, tried to straighten his legs. It was a hard exercise. He gave up and switched the radio on. "Fireflies" by Owl City. Marianne was working all day, and Rob had stopped by the flat to pick up his stuff and return the Robbie Williams CD. A rucksack on the floor held his possessions and he was finished here, but an air of melancholy kept him a while. An urge to eke out a few memories and a feeling he wouldn't be back. He twisted to reach the cupboard above his head and grabbed half a sliced loaf. A few more contortions and he added butter and raspberry jam from the fridge, and a plate and knife from a second cupboard— everything required for a jam sandwich. He contemplated the familiar surroundings. The Take That calendar on the wall filled with appointments, the oak table which made the kitchen such a focal point, the antique hat stand in the corridor, the permanently locked cellar door…. What was the point of finally getting a girlfriend if she finished with you after seven weeks and four days?

He spread the butter on a couple of slices of bread. A low-sided wooden bowl on top the opposite cupboard drew his attention. A clutter of items created an overflowing pile, including business cards, pens, lipstick—and a large black key. He hadn't noticed that before. Bruce Springsteen came on the radio—"Glory Days". He leapt from the sideboard, stretched for the bowl and, against better judgement, took the key.

Solid, black-riveted and scratched, the cellar door looked almost gothic, remaining from the time before the original house converted to flats, one of them Marianne's, and contrasting with the modern fixtures around it. The key worked and Rob pushed the door open. He pulled a light cord and descended a steep wooden staircase into a gloomy interior. A single bulb illuminated the whole cellar. The door creaked, above. A narrow passageway to the right terminated at an end wall, with boxes stacked two or three high against the crumbling side walls. A deep breath, and he headed left. The earthen floor kicked up dust as he walked.

Space the size of a medium garage opened up after a few yards. Books balanced the base of an exercise bike near one wall, and a couple of rolled up carpets leaned against the other. A wooden worktop dominated the area. Shadows of many shapes ran across its surface. A lamp towered to the right. He clicked the switch and was dazzled.

The lamp turned out to be a pair of spotlights, and his eyes needed several seconds to adjust. The worktop stood waist-high, designed for someone standing, and proved to be a modern piece of equipment. An array of shelves attached to the rear held labelled bottles of chemicals and flour-like parcels. Objects were grouped in separate islands on the desk, hinting at action yet to come. There were flasks, a microscope, several half pint-sized jars, test tubes in a rack, assorted glassware containing liquids, a formal notebook, and even a kind of mini-oven or kiln. Plus a CD player at the back right. In short, it was a laboratory. He flicked the notebook open. The heading on page one read "Project Hermes". Neat handwriting filled the rest of the page, logically structured with underlined subtitles and a summary diagram. An overview talked about inflammatory disease mechanisms and the goal of controlling or manipulating them. The cellar door slammed.

He sprinted to the stairs and made it halfway up before the door creaked open, only to shut again, more gently. A breeze, wherever that might be coming from. Relieved, he returned to the lab area. The jars contained a dark, sticky substance and he picked one up. Absently hefting it from hand to hand, a sweet cinnamon-type aroma floated into the atmosphere.

Marianne worked as a biochemist for a dairy company. She developed food processing methods to improve flavour and preservation, and her work involved a combination of computer modelling and laboratory testing. Rob first thought this lab was connected to her work in some way. Then again, he also knew she kept up to date with current research as a hobby—so maybe it served as an outlet for private study. The door slammed again and he took this as a sign to leave, switching the spotlights off on the way.

He locked the cellar and returned to the kitchen with the sample jar...still in his hand. He gave an "oh no" of exasperation and placed it on the table. He started to read the appointments on the calendar facing him. The March page showed Gary Barlow et al standing in a field. Today's date showed the start of a three-day break, highlighted with a smiley face—but had been crossed out. This should have been a long weekend on a Greek island. Rob was still going, alone, the flight from Southampton departing in three hours. Exactly what he needed—sunshine, snorkelling, a few beers, exploring the jungle-like interior. He might have read the brochure wrong on the jungle, but anyway, maybe he'd meet someone.

He moved the plate of bread and the jam from the sideboard to the table and sat down. A calendar entry for next Tuesday, 30 March drew his attention—"Roger". An identical entry marked the twenty-third. And the twentieth. He turned to April—the group playing frisbee on a beach—and found Roger again, on the first Saturday, accompanied by another smiley face. Roger was the name of their tennis club captain.

Rob sat down, spread the jam and took a bite. Hmmm…a strong hint of cinnamon. He was halfway through the sandwich before realising he'd actually spread the sample from the lab. He cleared up, put the jar back in the cellar and re-locked the door. The sandwich had tasted edible; he shrugged and threw the remainder in the bin. "Brown Eyed Girl" came on the radio, and he heard it out before flicking the off switch and leaving.

Chapter 3

"Hi. Rob Griffin. Physio appointment with Scott at six o'clock."

"Hello. I'm afraid Scott's been called away. Someone else is available—Kate Jones, but she won't be free for another fifteen minutes. Will that be all right?"

"She'll have all his notes?"

"Oh yes."

"Ok, no problem. Scott's mentioned her. She drives the white sports car outside?"

"Indeed she does." The receptionist answered a call.

Rob was a week back from his holiday and the suntan held firm. He poured a drink from the water cooler and sat down opposite a table stacked with reading material. He chose last week's *Hampshire Chronicle* and flicked through, nothing much catching his interest. There was something about planning permission, an unqualified dentist treating patients, a catering competition, an evil supervillain menacing Winchester. He read the article on page seven by Jerome Laroche, whose byline identified him as "on exchange from our sister newspaper in Bordeaux".

Masked "superman" strikes again

Police were yesterday called to the City Museum, Winchester to attend an after-hours incident of high seriousness. Staff say a masked man gained access to the Venta Belgarum Gallery and stole part of the priceless Sparsholt mosaic. He escaped through the building and across the nearby Cathedral grounds "at unbelievable speed". Julie Shaw, the curator of the Venta Gallery, said: "The intruder came through the window—I don't know how, we're on the third floor. He wore a black mask and a cape he kept fiddling with. The mosaic is from a fourth-century Roman villa near the village of Sparsholt and the centre of our collection. We're devastated. He forced one section free—it's split into five sections—and put all the tiles into a sack. He sprinted off, knocking over half the exhibits. Mr Evans—sixty-three—tried to stop him, but was thrown aside. The place is a mess."

This is similar to the episode at the art gallery on Great Minster Street I reported last week. In this case also, a masked man created a disturbance and made his escape at "incredible speed", stealing a valuable oil painting. What is the connection and purpose to these events? Be aware that I will keep you informed.

"Rob?"

He drained his water and crossed to an open treatment room, where the physiotherapist waited. She was about five nine, slim and blonde, the hair shoulder length and straying round the front of her neck. He shook hands, twirling the empty plastic cup in his left hand. "Kate?"

She nodded. "Pleased to meet you Rob. I'm sorry Scott isn't here, but we have spoken about you before?"

"You have?"

"Yes—all of us in fact. We want you injury-free and charging about that tennis court soon. You've been coming here two years now?"

"Yes." He explained all about his injuries and the

treatments they'd tried. The cartilage op on the knee had worked, but there always seemed to be minor injuries and low-level pain somewhere about his body. Kate showed full attention and tapped her pen against her lips…which distracted him. He concluded with, "The thing is, Scott keeps me on the road with massage and exercises—so I can play sport—but we never find a permanent fix. We do fix things, but something else goes wrong."

"Scott described the history pretty much the same," Kate said. "He worked on the basis that there had been some deep initial injury, perhaps the left hip, which eventually caused multiple muscle compensations and biases. Given this, he had to peel away each layer of imbalance and weakness to rehabilitate the whole body. Despite improvements, your body has stubbornly resisted, so he hopes I can assess you from a fresh perspective and track down the missing piece of the puzzle." She paused. "How is the hip? And the knee? And the shoulder?"

"Um…they're all fine. Somehow my whole body started working properly about a week ago."

"That's brilliant. So you're here to tell me there's nothing wrong with you?"

"I know it's strange."

Kate put down her notes and leaned against the desk. "Our accountants will be worried," she said.

Rob laughed. "I'm sure something else will break soon."

"Let's examine you anyway. Can you undress, down to your boxers?"

He dropped the cup.

Kate studied his posture and put him through his paces with a series of exercises. She started with half squats, lunges and calf raises, and got tougher. Much tougher. He struggled to breathe at the end.

"That's amazing. Could you do those single leg squats before—with the same depth and control?"

"No, not at all."

"There doesn't seem to be any injury or muscle compensation now." Her voice quietened, almost talking to herself. "The movement is symmetrical, the strength and control is like one of our trainers. How could your body not only recover from the injuries, but end up with enhanced strength?" She shook her head and returned to normal volume. "I would like to understand what's happened here. Can you come back in about two weeks and we can monitor what's changed and I can run some more tests?"

As Rob dressed, Kate commented on a tennis ball-sized bruise on his right calf, patches of yellow and purple merging together. "How did you hurt your leg?" she said.

"It's a reaction to a lizard bite. I've just spent a few days in the Greek islands and did some exploring in the forest. I felt a sudden sting and saw this green lizard scooting away, about a foot long. All my energy died for a couple of days. The resort said no one else had ever had that experience."

"I'm impressed," she said. Smiled. "I hope you still managed to enjoy the break? And get a tetanus shot?"

"Yes and yes. I ended up relaxing and enjoying the sunshine. The idea was to escape after, well, splitting up with someone, and to try lots of sports like windsurfing. Then this lizard bit me on the first day. However, my injuries are much better now. You don't think there could be a connection?"

"I think, Rob, you've worked hard on the exercises, which has helped. There must be another contributing factor, which we need to discover. The lizard hypothesis is…unlikely."

"I do feel terrific—difficult to believe my injuries are fixed. I'm playing tennis at River Park in an hour and—though I always enjoy it—looking forward to the game so much more." He mimed a forehand stroke.

"Enjoy your match. You probably know Paul Martin at the club—if you run into him, can you say 'Hi' please?"

"Funnily enough I'm playing Paul, he's a good friend. Yes, I will. Many thanks for the session—I'll call in to book another."

Rob left the door ajar. Everyone had gone and the office was silent. Kate tidied up the filing and checked her phone. She decided she'd go for a run once she got home. Before leaving, she pressed the intercom to an empty reception. "Bring me some lizards," she said, with a quiet laugh.

*****

"What were you thinking of? You were supposed to be on the beach, catching the rays and impressing the ladies. Not wandering around the jungle."

They stood next to the clubhouse. The evening was grey and on the edge of cold, though Paul still wore shorts. He was about six foot, slightly taller and more heavily-built than Rob, and a year older. Rob had more and darker hair, though still above the collar. Marginally more likely to be cast in a Hollywood movie, he thought.

"It wasn't exactly the jungle," Rob said. "More dense forest. No one goes there, that's the real beauty. I found hidden glades and exotic trees, a clear stream that kept popping up, and the sunshine crept through the leaves and made these amazing patterns. There were all kinds of flora and fauna….."

"Which attacked you."

"Well one lizard, yes. I got lots of sympathy around the pool."

"Ah. So that was your plan."

They started warming up on court. After a while they made it competitive, but didn't play a formal match. They rallied continuously, each player lunging and stretching so as not to let the ball pass, not worrying if it was somewhat out—it made for a free-flowing game and a tough workout. They took a break after half an hour and chatted at the net.

"So, what happened with Marianne?" Paul said. "Have you seen her lately?"

"No, not since I got back." Rob practised his backhand swing. "She's quite intense, more than you'd expect from knowing her casually. But unpredictable as well—sometimes she almost wanted to save the world, others she could be flippant. She had this cute habit…." He tried a forehand. "When we split, she said…well, a few things, but the key seemed to be she was restless and looking for a kind of excitement she couldn't explain."

"Sounds like she doesn't know what she wants." Paul gave him a tap on the shoulder. "Tricky—may not be much you can do, mate."

"Yeah, you're probably right." Rob balanced the tennis racket upright on his fingers for a moment, then flicked and caught it. "I am exciting, aren't I?"

"Sure." A pause. "We're all on a gradient—somewhere between James Bond and collecting dental floss. You're in the middle with the rest of us."

Rob smiled. "Slightly on the James Bond side, I hope. By the way, I just had a physio session with Kate Jones. She says 'hello'. You know her?"

"Kate? Yes, we met at a business networking event about three years ago. We got quite close—almost went out, but, for various reasons…didn't. I must have mentioned her. She is lovely."

Claire and David arrived on the adjacent court, an older couple who regularly played at the club, and they swapped greetings and a "starting to get dark, floodlights need to come on soon."

They returned to their respective baselines and resumed playing. Rob paused a moment as the conversation from their neighbours carried, David speaking. "Roger's a true gentleman. Gave me some tips the other evening. Brilliant player, of course."

Claire joined in. "Superb. He'll be going for the Hampshire Cup again this summer. That will be his fourth…fifth…."

Rob remembered Marianne's calendar entries, and, next shot he got, blasted the ball. Paul barely laid a racket on it. That set the scene for a shift in pattern. Rob increasingly moved quicker to the ball and periodically hit much harder—though not too often, as he tended to miss the court. He felt like he was experimenting with unfamiliar skills. Paul was the better player and still won more points, virtue of Rob's misses, but, after a while, Rob reached every shot outside a couple of well-disguised drop shots. Paul changed his tactics and threw a few lobs into the mix. Rob smashed the first into the net, the second for a winner, and the third headed straight over the baseline, knocked a hole in the fence and disappeared into the bushes.

"What the…" Paul said. "That's a new fence. What's happened? How come you're so much quicker? And hitting harder?"

Rob was puzzled himself, but put forward his tentative thinking. "My theory is all the injuries clearing up means my whole body is working better, all the muscles are reinforcing each other. I can't remember being injury free, well, forever. This could be a chance to fulfil my sporting potential."

"Wimbledon?"

"Is it too late to enter?" Rob said. "Seriously, some strange things are happening. I can run much faster. This is going to sound weird, but the way the timing works, I think the lizard bite has had an effect."

"Er, you think so? How fast are you talking?"

"I'm not sure. Shall we go for a run in the next couple of days—perhaps try a few sprints as well—see if it's all in my imagination?"

They agreed to meet the next evening, finished their game, left the courts, and headed to The Hyde for a beer. "What was Marianne's cute habit?" Paul said.

Chapter 4

Friday lunch hour. Sunshine and a light breeze played with the sports pitches at North Walls Recreation Ground. They were in mid-conversion from rugby to cricket for the summer. Kate was early and leaned against a tree bordering the far pitch, relishing the warmth. She opened yesterday's *Hampshire Chronicle*, the latest from Jerome Laroche on page three.

Masked menace vandalising Winchester

Again I am here to tell you the mysterious masked man has struck not once in the last week, not twice, but three times. Last Saturday, 3 April, a break-in occurred at the St Cross Hospital Almshouse. A two-foot-wide eighteenth-century pewter serving plate was stolen from the Medieval Kitchen in the Brethren's Hall, a trail of broken doors left behind. Brother Christopher Wilks was the only witness, spying our masked man leaving the hall at 10:30 p.m. As is now familiar the man left at high speed, our witness saying he flew to the top of the south wall and away; but that is scarcely credible, and Brother Wilks had been returning from the Bell Inn.

He chose Tuesday to strike next. Dean Garnier Garden in the Inner Cathedral Close is a tranquil sanctuary at the heart of Winchester, enclosed by medieval walls and on the site of a thirteenth-century monks' dormitory. A young couple, who wouldn't give their names, were alone in the garden at 2:00 p.m. and reported a caped man leaping through the ancient doorway and up the steps. He ran to a stone bench and wrenched free the curled dog sculpture underneath, before departing "like a whirlwind".

There were many more witnesses on Wednesday evening. The scene was the High Street at seven o'clock, under the Town Clock on the Lloyds Bank building. A figure balanced on the three hundred-year-old timber brackets and tried to wrest the clock free. Amanda James, a local artist, described him as "medium to tall, wearing a dark cape with a hood, a mask over his eyes, black leggings and always moving". This time the man was to be denied and fled over the rooftops after the crowd shouted abuse, but not before leaving a clue for the police. A piece of his cloak—of charcoal velvet— tore off on the clock's metalwork and floated to the ground. Who is this Velvet Vandal? What will he target next?

"Having fun?"

"Hello Paul." Kate gave him a hug. "Why have you lured me here? Other than to show me something that will blow my professional mind."

"That's the gist of it. How's life? It's been a while"

"Busy. Practice going well and I'm making some innovations. Doing a course on neurological physiotherapy, which keeps me out of trouble. Still running."

"Anyone on"—Paul nudged her—"the horizon?"

"No, not meeting new people at the moment. Trying a bit of internet dating, but…well. How about you and Sarah?"

"Good. A whole new experience for me because of her son—hadn't realised how amazing kids were. I think he's getting used to me now, but still a bit suspicious." He rested his arm against the tree. "Rob should be here any moment."

"Ah yes—whose injuries have magically cleared up. I am puzzled."

"You're going to be a lot more puzzled in a minute."

Rob approached from the direction of the leisure centre, tailing off from a jog and hailing them. "Hi Paul. Hello Kate." She gave a wave. "Sorry to drag you out over lunch."

"Rob, why are you wearing a suit?" Paul said.

"I've got a job."

"This is meant to be a professional sporting demonstration."

Lines on the pitch still defined the rugby boundaries. Paul explained from try-line to try-line measured ninety metres, ten short of the maximum legal size. Adding on the distance from the path bordering the park gave a round hundred metres. To double check, he produced a tape measure and practised making a single metre stride. He then kept count as he led them to the far end. Rob described his job to Kate, "a product manager at an electronics company, but the usual struggle to keep up, zillions of emails and meetings" and added "may be time to try something new." She kept half an ear on Paul's count and agreed the distance was correct. Rob jogged back down the pitch.

"Ready with the stopwatch?" Paul said to Kate. He raised his arm and slammed it against a lifted knee, the signal for Rob to launch himself forward. He ran close to the line of trees with fluid motion, each arm and opposite leg in near perfect synchronisation. Kate couldn't judge the speed at first, but as he passed tree by tree, he tore the ground up, strides impossibly long, quads pumping, tie and jacket tail streaming behind. He was on them and over the line. "Stopwatch Kate," Paul shouted. Rob took twenty metres to skid to a halt. "What time do you get?" Rob lay on his back, gasping.

"Kate?" Paul said. She didn't say anything.

Rob recovered. "I felt even faster this time. When I push off, I'm propelled forward by my whole body, my foot barely touches down for the next stride." He started experimenting with his gait in slow motion, giving himself an exaggerated thrust.

"Kate?"

"Six seconds," she said.

"It was six and a half last…."

"Six seconds." Kate placed her hands on her head. A glance behind showed Rob taking practice jumps. "How on earth…."

"No idea. His theory is that the rehab exercises and treatment eventually triggered a tipping point, causing all his muscles to switch on properly and work in harmony. And then a lizard bite created a reaction that made everything super-efficient."

"He's obliterated the hundred metres world record."

"I know. It's not completely crazy though, it's not like he can—"

"Guys," Rob shouted from behind and above them. They turned. Speechless. Rob was streaking through the air. His angled trajectory took him over the river. He reached a height of about thirty feet and descended in a mirror image of his ascent, landing hard in the scrubland of Winnall Moors.

"—fly."

Three seconds of stillness, Rob hidden from sight. Four seconds…five…then a rustle of bushes, a snapping of a low-lying branch and he was airborne. His return path was straight towards them and Paul had to duck as Rob pointed his feet ahead and downwards, karate-style, hitting the ground and rolling several times. He raised himself onto hands and knees, and sprang up. "Need to work on the landing," he said.

Kate stayed motionless a number of seconds. She started to laugh out of sheer disbelief. "Can't change direction either," Rob said. She couldn't stop. Rob joined in.

Paul shrugged. A grin broke out, broadening rapidly. He pointed at Rob. "Your"—he could hardly get the words out— "suit"—which was shredded and splattered with mud and vegetation stains—"you've got to…go back…to work."

They gave in to it, gasping, falling to their knees, finally collapsing flat on their backs, laughter cascading around the sports field.

Chapter 5

Rob met them both at seven that evening at the Mucky Duck. Their plans had been pushed back to discuss what was, to put it mildly, a momentous development.

"What can I get you, Clark Kent?" Paul asked.

"Pint of lager please."

Rob and Kate sat on a sofa at a low table. Football showed on the big screen to their right, but it was a minor match and no one was watching.

"Rob, how are you?" Kate said.

"Physically superb, I've been waiting ages to be free of injury. I guess I didn't expect the pendulum to go straight past normal to superpower."

"What about inside, this must be so weird?"

"My mind is racing, Kate. What should I do with these powers?—everything from ignoring them to becoming a fully-fledged superhero is…hammering at my brain. Is my health at risk? Did a lizard really trigger this?"

Paul arrived with their drinks and joined them on the opposite side of the table. "Rob, what are you going to do?"

"I don't think he can know yet," Kate said. "There's so much to take in."

"I do have one idea—"

"You could become rich," Paul said. "The Olympics, Hollywood—"

"Quite a modest one—"

"We should assess your capabilities first," Kate said. "Measure performance, heart rate, pulse—"

"I'm going to win the Hampshire Cup."

"What?"

"The county tennis championships. Deadline for entries is next week. All you need is a Lawn Tennis Association rating—I got one last year. I'd start in the preliminary rounds because mine is low."

Paul paused and lowered his pint without taking a sip. "But…aside from other opportunities to consider…with respect Rob, you'd still need to play first-class tennis."

Rob leaned back and pointed at Paul. "Exactly," he said. "One of my dreams is to win a sports tournament. It has to be a real challenge to mean something. I can't just run the hundred metres in six seconds and pick up a medal."

Kate supported him. "Why not? It's an adventure. A chance to explore these powers without drawing everyone's attention. As long as you don't fly about the court."

"Yes," Rob said. "Of course a quality coach would be key. Someone who could make the most of my powers to actually improve the tennis. And a physio as well—you're right Kate, we need to monitor what my body is doing, if things are changing, strength and speed measurements." He drank from his pint. "You both in?"

Paul, head in hands, looked up and gave an exaggerated shrug. "Why not."

Kate smiled. "Me too. Physio and monitoring is on the house. I don't have many superheroes on the books."

They agreed to keep Rob's powers secret, and then discussed the ethics of trying to win a tennis tournament with superpowers. Rob hadn't knowingly taken any substances, wasn't at a high level of tennis anyway, and there was no monetary reward. The arguments weren't watertight but you had to live, and they were cool with it.

Paul drained his pint and stood, ready to leave. He mentioned the newspaper reports on Winchester's masked villain, wondering if Rob had a theory.

"Someone looking for attention or local notoriety," he suggested.

"One strange thing: I'm pretty sure all the places hit were part of your Year of Culture."

"Really?" Rob paused. "A coincidence, I guess. He's targeting well known landmarks."

"Yes, probably." Paul left, running late to meet his girlfriend.

Kate needed to go too, but stayed a few minutes. Rob found out that she was thirty-four, a year younger than Marianne. She'd been a physio for eight years and had travelled extensively in her early twenties. Before he could learn more, she leapt back to the earlier discussion. "What was your Year of Culture?"

"Last year my New Year's resolution was to do a cultural activity every week. Art galleries, plays, museums, Status Quo concerts…. Even though I sometimes scrambled desperately to find something at the end of the week, it's one of the best things I've done. I wrote a blog which you can find online."

"Status Quo—are you sure that's cultural?"

Rob paused as a cheer went up from the screen—someone had scored. "Believe me, some of the entries were dodgier. I did write them up a bit tongue in cheek, but I never failed to be engaged by each week's event."

"Sounds brilliant. What was the best one you did?"

"I struggle to answer this—all or none of them. The whole quest and mindset, I think: searching for an activity every week; turning up—often in trepidation—yet always becoming fascinated; researching and writing the blog. Maybe hiking out to see Juliet Turner at a Twickenham pub on a Sunday evening, or Liz Arnold's fantastic paintings, or the Peninsular Barracks and Military Museums in Winchester because that was the final one." Leaning forward and resting his arms on the table, he gave a rueful smile. "I feel a bit lost this year, as if some excitement's gone."

"Well you do have superpowers and the quest for the Hampshire Cup."

"Good point."

They said goodbye and Rob kissed her on the cheek, a touch of perfume staying with him. Floral, maybe jasmine.

He ordered another pint and drank it slowly, one elbow against the bar, scanning the pub's interior and taking in the atmosphere. You don't acquire superpowers every day.

Chapter 6

A couple of weeks later and Marianne was in her private lab. She switched from CD to radio. Twice through Take That's *Ultimate Collection* is enough for anyone, though the music only registered in the background. Her main focus was to understand the results of the model she had just run on the laptop. She leaned forward, elbows on the worktop. Half an eye stayed on a bubbling flask, the centrepiece of a series of chemical reactions which fed through glass tubing and added drip-wise to the contents. The spotlights illuminating the cellar threw odd shadows due to their off-centre positioning, creating a spooky feel which she liked (mostly).

This wasn't the main lab she used for her private project, of course. She enjoyed working down here, though—what better than the thrill of working in a secret lab for a fantastical project? Her time here largely consisted of writing up results and running software models. Experimental work was limited to minor modifications and testing. She also stored and catalogued samples and prototypes, with a variety of jars and packages lodged on the shelves. This reminded her, she needed to check on Rob. Elementary detective work, relating to a sandwich in a bin, told her, unbelievably, he had eaten some of sample K28. She didn't expect any obvious effects but maybe some minor physiological changes.

It was ten o'clock on Saturday morning and, after three hours work, her concentration wandered. She checked her phone. No new messages but the last text confirmed tennis with Roger at eleven. Probably a drink afterwards, although hadn't Roger mentioned the sports exhibition at the library?

Forcing herself back to the laptop, she gave up on the model and started writing some notes. She meant to turn these into a report for her benefactor before the weekend ran out. The reports weren't mandatory, but she didn't want any risk of losing the support she received—not least access to a state of the art genetics lab in Oxford. A scrabbling sound to the left distracted her further, as the cat stirred and cast about for some imagined creature.

She tidied up the experiment and powered down the laptop. On her way out she crouched and ruffled the cat's coat, and nudged him towards the stairs. "Come on, Spot," she said. A snack beckoned, followed by tennis and the rest of the day.

*****

"Full English please, and a bottle of orange juice." Rob bounded up the stairs at Blues Café to wait for a late breakfast. Tennis had gone well that morning—an hour of drills at the Kingsgate courts, superbly set amongst the water meadows by the Itchen Navigation. Paul's coaching centred on Rob using his speed to always get to the right position to strike the ball. Despite not having technically good strokes this gave an enormous advantage, providing the time to play a purer shot or at least make a deep return. Preliminary round one of the Hampshire Cup pitted him against Arthur McDonald. The match was at two this afternoon, his confidence high.

He sat on a high stool facing the window and studied the street below. An open top sports car queued at the traffic lights, tempted out by the spring sunshine. The car reminded him of Kate, not that he knew much about cars or even if it was the same type as hers. Shortly after the traffic lights changed, a man, accompanied by a boy of about ten, entered the barber shop opposite. A cat sat in the window of the house above and to the left of the barber's, not doing much.

That was about it, so he picked up a folded paper on the window shelf, and found it was Thursday's *Hampshire Chronicle*. Jerome Laroche had graduated to the front page.

Winchester Round Table stolen: Velvet Vandal strikes again

Unbelievable. Inconceivable. One of Winchester's greatest monuments is stolen. Appropriated. Nicked. How can this be possible? The Great Hall is a magnificent thirteenth-century stone arena with soaring roof and ancient flagstones and pillars. Go there towards dusk and you can almost see medieval banquets astir, oil lamps flickering, vast carcasses of meat, serving wenches with flagons of beer, drunken revelry. Enough imagining. Pride of place in the Great Hall is the ancient Round Table hanging on the wall: a one-ton, five-metre-wide oak table depicting King Arthur's knights. And it has vanished.

Sebastien Martin of Hampshire County Council, the custodian of the Hall, arrived at 6:00 a.m. Wednesday to find the massive doors swinging in the wind. As he advanced inside he was stunned by the gap on the wall where the Table should have been. Some of the wooden fastenings lay broken on the floor, and scratches marked parts of the floor and columns. Otherwise no clue seemed apparent as to what had occurred. Mr Martin immediately called the police, who are baffled by events. But they found one clue—a patch of charcoal velvet attached to the falcon statue in the adjoining Queen Eleanor's Garden. Inspector Giles Hunter gave the following statement and called for witnesses: "We are struggling to make sense of this. A person or persons unknown has broken into the Great Hall, removed a one ton monument from high on the wall and spirited it away without anyone noticing. I am confident we will solve this: this is the theft of a priceless local artefact and is being treated with the highest priority." The inspector went on to say that the velvet fabric could suggest a link with other events reported by this paper, but this was on a different scale entirely. He appealed for anyone who saw or heard anything on the night of Wednesday 14 April to contact him. Hampshire County Council have offered a two thousand pound reward for information leading to the return of the Round Table.

To my thinking the Velvet Vandal must surely be the culprit? This time no witnesses tell the tale, but the trademarks of speed, the rapid gain of height, and a certain boldness are evident here and perhaps we have underestimated this dastardly villain.

"Ah, just here please," Rob said, moving the paper and smiling at the waitress as she placed his breakfast on the table. He reread the article while eating and recalled memories of the research he had done for his Year of Culture. The Great Hall formed the centrepiece of a rich area of culture adjacent to Winchester law courts. The remnants of Winchester Castle sat next to the hall. From the Hall itself, one door led to Queen Eleanor's Garden, a recreation of a medieval garden, and another to a historic art gallery in the Council offices behind.

There was also the modern Hampshire Jubilee Sculpture in the courtyard, and Peninsula Barracks and the military museums weren't far away. Rob liked the Round Table. He was intrigued, and starting to get annoyed. He shrugged it off and left to prepare for his match and whatever else the day would bring.

*****

Paul expected an imminent business call, and, at the same time, was trying to prepare lunch and keep Liam entertained. Sarah had left precise instructions, but did you really need them to feed a five-year-old?

He appreciated the chance to spend more time with Sarah's son. He wanted him to be comfortable with him and thought he was gradually getting there. Liam's biological father lived away, in Manchester, and saw him every second weekend and otherwise on arrangement. Sarah had kept things flexible since the split, two years ago, and Liam had adapted well to the situation—though showed a wariness to men not his father.

"Fish fingers please," Liam said, sitting patiently at the kitchen table.

"That's not what your mum's written here. It says chicken quesadilla, sweetcorn salsa and raw carrots."

"What's a quesadill?"

Paul's mobile rang, the display confirming the expected call. Kelly Smith, his potential client, ran a national adventure travel company based in London. Paul had been wooing her for months and felt convinced an order would propel his startup to the next level. "Some kind of bread, I think," he said. He answered the phone.

"One second please," he said to Kelly.

He muted the phone and said "Can you play with your colouring puzzles while I'm on the phone, and I'll sort everything out in a minute?"

He returned to Kelly. "Your email said the trial went well, do you have some data you can share...ok excellent. We can tweak the parameters and squeeze out one final improvement. I'll ask Ravi to work on it." She was fine with that and moved on to the licensing costs. "Well, you know our situation and that we're early in the product cycle. Your satisfaction and adoption is more important than initial price." Three months to get to this stage, and although a large order would be cause for celebration, having a client that could be used as a reference was his main aim. "And of course you're our favourite customer!" A little banter passed to and fro, and then a pause as she checked some online data.

Paul turned the chicken strips over one-handed, phone still to his ear. He found the quesadilla packet and put it on the table, stopping behind Liam to study his colouring scene. "Is that a tiger?"

"Yes." Liam pointed at other outlines. "And a bear. And a snake." Ah...The Jungle Book. "Who are you talking to?"

"It's my customer from London. I'm trying to sell—" Kelly interrupted and they finished their conversation, agreeing to meet and (hopefully) finalise things the week after next.

Efficiency software was the product Paul and his partner Ravi were trying to build a business on. A quick google search on "how to be efficient at work" would throw up a variety of ideas like switch off email for periods to avoid being distracted, set priorities and task lists for each day, work out the most efficient order for tasks, a proper filing system, clear communication, take breaks. Ravi had developed software to help enforce this, subject to user preferences. It would, for example, hide email for periods, prompt for task lists, provide an organisation tool and highlight long-winded text. There were a few clever tricks, but mostly workers were nudged to do something they could do for themselves given discipline. Initial trials gave impressive results.

Paul moved into culinary action, and considered how to explain his business. Chicken done and placed on the table, salsa dip found in the fridge, carrots washed, and a surprise extra—a tub of cheese spread making up for the lack of fish fingers. "My friend Ravi and I have invented something our customer wants to buy. It's something that, er, helps them concentrate…so they can work harder."

Liam watched him shred a quesadilla, trying to spread the cheese spread. "Like a robot helmet?"

"Yes, sort of. One you can take off when you want."

Though the conversation kept some formality, Paul managed to steer between tigers, dinosaurs and football, and earn one laugh (for his tyrannosaurus rex impression). Despite seeing Liam's mother for over a year, he had only spent any real time with him in the last three months or so. Initially, just seeing Sarah had suited him, but now—and this had crept up on him—he looked forward to time with Liam. Today had gone well, he thought.

Sarah would be back in an hour and the afternoon was ahead of him. "Do you want to watch Football Focus?" he said.

*****

Kate stirred her coffee for the seventh time. Don't judge

too soon, she urged herself. He's outside his usual habitat, trying to impress; and there is a dash to his looks and movie-style hair.

"That reminds me," Arnold said, flicking his hair. "When I was in Singapore—the bank sent me to help out a finance restructure for our client...that was a good deal, six figure bonus. Point of the story is, round the block from my offices was this extraordinary rooftop café. Circular bar, great views of the city, 138 different types of coffee bean and get this—they roasted the beans in the shop."

"Wow."

"Management beckoned afterwards. I run one of our Control divisions in Reading, but I spend a week each month in Chicago. Did I mention that?"

"Yes. Twice."

"Ha. Sorry, I've talked about me. You're a physiotherapist aren't you? Do you try and change the status quo in your work?"

Ok, an interesting...challenge. He leaned back, looked directly at her. "In a way. Let me give you an example. Say you have an Achilles injury. For a ruptured tendon, for example, you'd need surgery, but usually the injury appears over time and becomes a chronic problem. Once the pain subsides, the key is strength training. The research shows eccentric exercise is best for long-term recovery."

"You mean like working out dressed as a pirate?" He grinned at her and slouched a bit further into his chair.

Kate sighed, but gave a small smile as well. "Sure, or exercising...with your pet parrot. No, seriously, eccentric exercises mean those that work the muscle as it lengthens. For example, rising on tiptoe is concentric. The muscle tenses as the calf shortens. Lowering the heel off a step—a heel drop—is eccentric." She stood up and demonstrated. "The patient needs the right program to gradually increase the intensity and return to sporting activities."

"Would the parrot have to do the same workout? Or would it have special parrot exercises?"

"Never mind the parrot," she said. "With the Achilles, strengthening the area is only half the answer. You need to identify the root cause and address that as well—could be a weak hip, poor foot strike, overtraining. I manage the patient through all this." She paused and smiled. "That'll be twenty pounds please."

"I can see your passion," he said. "It reminds me, when I was in Japan—"

"Which can wait just a second." She pointed at him, kind of playfully. "The thing is, muscular injuries can be highly complex and have knock-on effects through the body. One problem for the patient is they're faced with so many different types of professionals and techniques: physiotherapy, sports massage, osteopathy, muscle activation—fixing muscles that don't switch on because the brain's got used to restricted patterns of movement, even acupuncture…. And there's often no agreed protocol for an injury."

"There's not?"

"No. Anyway, I'm working with a local group of sports injury professionals. The idea is to create a forum to discuss and document the best approach for the most common musculoskeletal problems—the correct initial treatment and exercise regime, how to identify the root cause, options when it's not working, when to refer to a specialist."

"You're writing a book?"

"A website. What's good is we're from a mix of disciplines so we're learning a lot from each other's perspectives. The number one rule is to have open minds." She finished her coffee. "Sorry, I'm talking too much."

"No, I'm fascinated, Kate. What's clear is physiotherapy and similar professions need to be managed right from the top. I'm sure people are dedicated, but it sounds like a struggle in the dark. In a well-run company someone would be in charge of a different research or operational area; then someone should run a group of these areas, finding efficiencies and the right answers; and so on, up to the CEO."

"You mean like with Enron? Or a number of dictatorships round the world? Surely, flexibility and informal collaboration can often cut through to the solution."

Arnold sat up straight and looked at Kate. "Fair point. A bit hit and miss, though. The company—or profession or country—just has to be run right, with proper control and direction."

"Um…how are you finding this dating site, Arnold?"

"Everyone's friendly and interesting in their own way. I've inter—er, met five women. What I need is the right amount of chemistry and someone who'll fit in with my lifestyle."

"I'm looking for tall, dark and handsome."

Arnold studied his watch. "Apologies, Kate. Another appointment. You've been compelling—I'll be in touch." He stood, leaned over and kissed her on the cheek, put a tenner on the table and, with a final flick of the hair, was gone.

The rest of the afternoon awaited her, but first Kate ordered another coffee and tried not to laugh.

Chapter 7

"Congratulations," Paul said, reaching out to shake hands. "Through to the first round proper."

"Thanks to your excellent coaching. 6-4 6-4 in the end but I felt comfortable."

Sunday lunchtime found them in the narrow sun-speckled beer terrace of the Bakers Arms. The barmaid brought cheese rolls to go with their pints. They talked about yesterday's match and training strategies. Rob had drawn another qualifier in the first round, but would face a huge test against the number two seed in the following round if both won. Roger, the top seed, was the other side of the draw so they couldn't meet until the final.

Paul shifted his chair to better catch the sun and changed the subject. "Heard from Marianne at all?" he asked.

"Yes, she sent a text yesterday—wanted to know about my health and if I'd been feeling different lately."

"Spooky—surely she can't suspect anything? What did you say?"

"I haven't replied."

"Still a bit raw?"

Rob adjusted his chair. "Um. I am disappointed—everything seemed fine. I…miss her, although current events are a big distraction. I went flying last night"—he simulated an airplane with his hand—"but more on that later. Not sure whether to try and win her back."

"Do you think you could?"

"Ah, well. The Internet tells me how to win a girlfriend back."

"Er…go on."

"The foundation is the no contact rule. No texts, no accidental meetings, no replying to her messages. The theory is she'll miss you and wonder what you're doing. Part B is self-improvement. Start going down the gym and shape up, socialize—be photographed with Hollywood actors or fashion models, quit your dead end job and land a top executive position. Then make contact: casually lean against a wall as she's passing and say 'hi' with a raise of the eyebrow."

"And she'll swoon," Paul said. They both laughed. "Seriously though, you do now have superpowers."

"True. Not sure what she'd make of that. Given she's made this decision I think I need to move on, but…." He finished his cheese roll. Sipped his pint. "Talking of superpowers, I'm meeting Kate for some physio tests in a couple of hours."

"Now Kate is attractive."

"I have noticed, and fun and intelligent. She has these eyes that light up when she laughs, hazel with flecks of blue…. Anyway, she's trying online dating—had a date yesterday. Do you think I have a chance?"

Paul finished his pint. "There's always that Rob. Kate's genuine, nice. When we were close she was searching for a purpose, but I think she's found it with the innovations she's driving at her physio practice. Maybe she's ready to meet someone. Pretty selective, though."

"Oh well," Rob said, with a mock sigh.

They left the pub and headed towards the second-hand bookstall in the porch at the back of the Cathedral. Paul wanted a book for Liam, perhaps something on dinosaurs.

"So, about your flying?"

"Ah yes." Rob pulled a mask from his pocket and placed it

over his head. "I don't want stories appearing in the *Hampshire Chronicle*, so I go out at night—usually over the Downs beyond St Catherine's Hill. But in case I'm spotted, this is to prevent identification." The mask, consisting of dark green stretch material, framed his eyes and covered his nose and upper cheek.

"Good grief." Paul stared. "You're going to need a superhero name. The Green…I'll come up with something. Rob, you could become a genuine crime fighter."

"No. That's much too clichéd. I need to find something that feels right. After last year, maybe something linked to culture—though I can't think what at the moment." They passed the front of Winchester Cathedral and turned left through the side passage towards Cathedral Close. "Take this area. The culture is so rich. Apart from the Cathedral itself, Dean Garnier Garden is on the site of the dormitory of St Swithun's Priory—a Benedictine monastery dissolved in the 1500s. The Deanery and the stunning porch with the bookstall is thirteenth century. Pilgrim's Hall—part of Pilgrim's School—has the world's earliest hammer beam roof and no, I don't know what that is either. Priory Gate, the massive fifteenth-century entrance doors they still shut each night—"

As they approached the high stone arches in front of the bookstall, a fire engine raced through Priory Gate and pulled to a stop by an elm tree in the corner of the green. The area was otherwise quiet, a few people dotted around. A fireman dismounted to talk to a woman who pointed halfway up the tree. A cat perched in the fork between a branch and the trunk. They crossed the green to investigate.

"…been there since yesterday," the woman was saying. "They said she'd find her own way down, but she hasn't." Mid-fifties and dressed in jeans, jacket and a scarf whose ends fluttered in the breeze, she leaned against a crutch held in her right hand.

"Trouble is, cats like to climb forwards, but they can't when they're coming down, their claws won't hold 'em. Sometimes they're scared to come down backwards." The fireman raised his arm and squinted along it, adjusting the angle until he pointed exactly at the cat. "About forty feet," he said. "We're not meant to attend this sort of thing, but the station's quiet today."

Behind him, the whole cab started signalling.

"Tricky to put the ladder up there. We could hose her down." The woman stared at him, and he hastily amended, "Only joking…"

One of the crew twisted himself out the cab and shouted, "Geoff—a call out."

"Sorry love, didn't mean to make fun, we've got to go. Call the RSPCA." A couple of strides and a leap up the steps, and then a screeching reverse by the fire engine. A swift exit followed, retracing its original path.

"Useless," the woman said. "So frustrating." She raised her crutch and banged the ground. She took a deep breath, "Sorry, I'm Cynthia," she said, "and the cat's Ella."

Paul gave a wide smile and shook her left hand "Paul," he said. "They should have shown more respect. We can call the RS…"

"I'll get your cat down," Rob said.

Cynthia looked at Rob—still disguised by the mask—and then the tree. The lowest branch was twelve feet above them.

Rob backed away, took a run up and scrambled his way up the trunk. A push off with his left hand gave him the momentum to catch the branch with his right, and he pulled himself on top.

"Who the heck is he?" Cynthia said.

Six people had congregated a few steps behind them—a couple and their two young sons, a middle aged vicar and a teenage boy. An old man shuffled towards the group. "Er, my friend," Paul said, looking up and generally around.

"But what's he called?" the teenager said.

Rob accelerated from a crouching start, finding enough purchase each maneuvre to propel himself upwards and he gained the next branch in seconds. A cry of "careful" rang out, mixed with some indistinct chatter, and then the vicar yelled "Come on son."

The tree structure grew more complex and easier to climb, and Rob gained the branch beneath the cat. The crowd, swelled to twelve now, cheered. Rob half-knelt, half-stood, leaning against the trunk. He inched an arm towards the cat and spoke softly, "Hello Ella." She hissed, and managed to arch her back while still low to the branch, claws digging in. Rob hesitated.

"How you gonna get 'er down, mister?" came from the teenager below.

Rob shot out his right arm, grabbed Ella by the scruff of the neck, lifted her and tried to pull her to his chest. The claws slashed wildly, tangling with his shirt and scratching through. He rapidly moved her to arm's length, on the edge of falling. His other hand pressed hard against the trunk and he stabilised. As long as he didn't move, the claws couldn't reach him. The struggles became more intermittent, giving some respite. He shouted down in the direction of Cynthia, "Can I hold her like this?"

"Yes, just get her down quickly." Panic in her voice.

He looked at the downclimb—harder than coming up, only one free hand and a struggling animal. He shouted down again, "Paul, if anything goes wrong, you'll have to catch her."

Paul took a couple of hesitant steps forward. "It's got claws…"

Rob inched his left shoulder down the trunk, smeared his left hand against any purchase he could find and cautiously lowered his feet. Paul gave directions—"Right foot to your right and down, you'll feel the branch." Rob made the branch and took a breath, cat still out of reach but calm for a second. He tried to repeat the trick to the next branch. Halfway, Ella lashed out, enough to unbalance him, and he fell into it, ending up spread-eagled, cat struggling like wildfire, staring at the ground twenty-five feet below. He forced himself onto his left side, grip precarious. The cat scratched and squirmed round his back and there was no way he could hold on. With a final twist and kick, she broke free and was airborne, and Rob reinforced his grip.

Paul watched closely and leaned back, bracing himself. The cat took just over a second to fall. She hit him in the chest, claws first. He fell backwards, cushioning the impact, hands loosely cradling the cat.

Ella darted off, changing direction several times. Eventually she went to ground behind a second, nearby tree and allowed Cynthia to scoop her up. Rob climbed down with no further incident, jumping from the lowest branch and rolling as he hit the ground. He pulled Paul to his feet and they faced the crowd.

"Get in there," the vicar said, and pumped his fist. One by one the crowd started to clap. The applause lasted a full thirty seconds. Several phone cameras captured the scene—a mysterious green-masked man and his associate with a scratched neck.

Paul stretched his arm towards Rob. "This," he said, "is Culture Man."

Chapter 8

"You'll appreciate I'm taking these measurements in a detached clinical manner and ignoring the fact they're crazy."

Rob let out a breath as he recovered from the T-Test. This measured agility by forcing rapid changes of direction as he sprinted between a series of cones arranged in a T shape. They were in the grassy park of Oram's Arbour, a few hundred yards from Kate's home. "Are there patterns that stand out, Kate?"

She finished writing on a clipboard and nodded. "Performance testing can be split by function. There are different ways to do this, but I'm considering five areas: strength and power, speed, endurance, agility and proprioception or balance."

"Flying?"

"We don't usually test that." She played with a smile and put the stopwatch in her tracksuit pocket. "Sticking with the conventional categories, speed and agility are phenomenal. Strength is impressive, double what's expected, but the change hasn't kept pace with your speed. You wouldn't win a weight lifting contest like you'd win the Olympic hundred metres. Proprioception has improved, but I suspect only due to the other changes, not inherently. Endurance, we need to test more. The performance appears to diminish with time, because—whatever this is—it drains you. I think you could run the mile in about four minutes, but I'm not sure we'll find any advantage in marathon-type activities."

"Yes, that rings true. I recover quickly, but I'm exhausted for a few seconds. So something like tennis is fine, I can rest between the rallies." He paused mid-stretch. "Maybe I can win a marathon with stop-start super sprints, gasping like mad in between."

"So much to discover Rob, but we're going to uncover how this is working and what your body is actually doing—including the flying. We can do some sensory tests back at the house, well vision anyway, I'm still trying to borrow some hearing test kit. We'll have to establish if your powers are changing with time. And then…," she stopped herself. "Timeout. Enough craziness for a moment, let me calm my brain." She sat on the adjacent bench and lounged back. "So, Culture Man, any more cats to rescue today?"

Rob raised his arms in an exaggerated shrug. "I was hoping not to draw attention to myself."

"Well, you're wearing a mysterious mask, you approach a distressed woman and say 'I'll rescue your cat', and you proceed to save the day and pose for the cameras."

"You make a fair point. Think it'll get in the *Chronicle*?" Kate nodded. "At least I didn't fly."

"Which we need to talk about," Kate said. "I'm trying to think how best to monitor your body on take-off, but—"

"A video would be fantastic to start—"

"First of all, there's a huge safety issue. We don't understand any of the parameters here. You could drop out of the sky."

"Yes, understood. Somehow it doesn't feel dangerous. I need some kind of launch pad—usually the ground—to…propel myself and accelerate. After that the sensation is more like gliding, though my body has to stay tense. I am careful, I've never flown longer than a minute yet."

"Even so."

"You'd miss me if I ended up in a man-shaped crater?"

"Of course." She stood and gathered her clipboard. "How would I finish my Nobel-winning paper?"

They strolled through the late afternoon towards Kate's residence, a modern semi-detached house. Sunshine still warmed them through gaps in the hedges and walls. Fitful birdsong sounded, a cyclist breezed past and a man and dog passed on the other side the road. They walked without talking until Rob broke the silence at the garden gate. "How did your date go?"

"Aaargh."

"Good then?"

"Arnold…I'll try not to be unfair…he had a presence, he was polite, intelligent. But give men some confidence, why are they so arrogant, so self-obsessed."

Rob opened his mouth but didn't reply.

Kate paused at the front door, key in hand. "He thought he could solve all the questions of physiotherapy by imposing some management structure. And don't get me started on his general brilliance…"

"Perhaps he was nervous, trying to impress."

"Hah."

"Women can be quite demanding you know, Kate." She looked at him, expression somewhere between pursed lips and a smile. Rob had a smile and a hand held up. "I wasn't there, but devil's advocate: If I meet someone, say in a bar—the thing women always say they want is confidence. So you have to be note perfect. Cool, casual, brilliantly amusing conversation. Ideally save her from some mortal danger. Then for the follow-up—texts, dates—you need to keep up this James Bond persona. And I'd probably have to be able to cook."

Kate laughed and shook her head.

Once inside, they tried out an online eye examination which had been recommended by an optometrist friend. Rob easily passed every test. Afterwards, Kate tried to find his limits. She pulled up a cookery site and used the zoom to shrink the text to twenty percent, creating an unreadable blur. Rob read out the recipe for fish pie, followed by chicken soup at fifteen percent, finally failing with rhubarb crumble at ten percent.

"Unbelievable." Kate typed the results into a spreadsheet and began to add the earlier notes from her clipboard. "What are you going to do with these powers?"

"Paul and I spoke about that earlier. He suggested a kind of traditional crime fighting role, in jest I think. Not sure whether he was thinking Superman or Hong Kong Phooey. I dismissed the idea, but…a couple of things come to mind. One, the ideas that scare you are sometimes the ones worth doing. And two, pretty much every kid has wanted to be a detective at some point. Set up an agency, solve people's problems…which by a series of coincidences will lead to glamorous international cases."

"In Winchester? You're not seriously thinking about this?"

"No, not really," he said. Slowly, with hesitation. "Something else, slightly related—remember the other day, Paul mentioned the Velvet Vandal targeting the places from my culture blog. The idea's ridiculous, but…it's nagged at me. I'll do some research and cross-check the crimes."

They discussed activities for the next session before Rob left about six, both of them with chores to do, the weekend counting down to Monday morning. As he opened the door, Kate nudged his arm. "What you said about men needing to be perfect for women—you do know that's not true?"

*****

Rob raced up the three flights of stairs to his flat in the St Cross area of Winchester. A glow from the day showed no sign of departing. He ran a mental checklist: cat rescued; time with Kate and, he thought, plenty of rapport; superpowers showing no sign of fading; a bold plan in mind; and—checking the online schedule—Doctor Who on catch-up TV. Superb.

First job was to check the Velvet Vandal crimes against his blog. He could send Kate an email with the results. He pulled up two windows on the PC, one showing his Year of Culture blog and the other an archive of the *Hampshire Chronicle*. Initially he went from memory, not needing to check the *Chronicle*. There was the theft of an oil painting from the gallery on Great Minster Street—and yes, week one described his visit to The Minster Gallery. He read through his blog post, which described the Rod Pearce Exhibition of oil paintings on display at the time. Next was the theft from the Medieval Kitchen at St Cross Hospital. He scanned through his blog looking for an equivalent entry, but inevitably got distracted.

Week 5 (26 Jan-1 Feb): Southampton City Art Gallery

Desperate times—2:00 p.m. on Sunday and no culture so far. Surely I couldn't fail in week 5. Luckily for the blog, no. Bike, train and a semi-jog brought me to Southampton City Art Gallery for three o'clock, an hour before closing. A quick look round the main gallery left me uninspired. Many pictures were superbly painted but they soon merged into a kind of sameness, nothing crying for attention. My quest is to be engaged and not just go through the motions. A sign pointing to eight more galleries caused my heart to sink, but I trudged onwards—and then two pictures saved me:

George Shaw's "Scenes from the Passion: The Unicorn": George Shaw's Scenes from the Passion is a series of paintings from the Tile Hill estate in Coventry, where he grew up in the 1970s. He uses Humbrol enamels which are used for painting airplane models, resulting in glossy reflective pictures. What stands out is partly the sheer detail but, more so, that the scenes are deliberately depopulated—there are no characteristics to identify the location, no people, signs or vehicles—which gives a fascinating eerie quality. I saw a quote that said he was trying to recreate the memories of his youth by removing recent additions to the scene, and that—brilliantly poignant, this—for each youthful moment he can recall (and paints) he mourns thousands forgotten. I first thought it was a house and drive, but The Unicorn is a picture of an estate pub.

LS Lowry's "July, the Seaside": Many people will remember the song by Brian and Michael about Lowry, "Matchstalk Men and Matchstalk Cats and Dogs", and its references to Salford's smokey tops and Ancoats (a district of Manchester). A great song ruined by the kids singing on it—the same thing happened with Clive Dunn's Grandad, but I digress. Anyway, I'd never seen an LS Lowry painting that I could recall. "July, the Seaside", painted in 1943, showed a seaside scene, as you'd expect, with just so much going on. There were about two hundred adults and children all doing different things, plus cats, dogs, prams, swings, boats, horses and further activities at the horizon you couldn't make out. All this detail…but when you look closely all you find is a matchstalk figure. I loved it. For the briefest of biographies: LS Lowry produced about a thousand paintings and eight thousand sketches, many of northern industrial scenes, especially Salford; he worked as a rent collector until retirement at sixty-five, keeping his job a secret from the public; the largest collection of his work is displayed at The Lowry, Salford Quays; he died in 1976 at eighty-eight.

Moving on, Rob found the entry for St Cross Hospital in week nine.

Week 9 (23 Feb-1 Mar): St Cross Hospital / Winchester football

I had the lads (Sean and Duncan) down for the weekend. They were keen to sample whatever culture I could find as long as it didn't interfere with the Six Nations rugby showing at the Exchange. St Cross Hospital is about half a mile down the road from me, and we headed there on the Saturday afternoon. Our interest had been piqued by the Wayfarer's Dole, an ancient tradition providing a goblet of ale and a portion of bread for visitors—but only if you ask for it at the Porter's Gate. We availed ourselves of this on arrival; for the record, the beer is London Pride. The hospital is a medieval almshouse founded in 1132 and supports a community of "Brothers". The building is superb. Once you pass through the Porter's Gate, you're in the Inner Quadrangle This is surrounded by a stunning twelfth-century Norman church with Purbeck Marble columns to the fore, private apartments for the twenty-five Brothers on the right, a fifteenth-century hall and medieval kitchen behind you, and a Tudor cloister on the left which leads to a large and tranquil garden—all set in the picturesque St Cross meadows. The Brothers are given flats in the grounds, pay a rent depending on ability and have to attend church daily. Catherine, the porter, was very informative and patient with our queries, including those on how to become a Brother. Basically, they should be over sixty years old and unattached. Preference is given to those most in need but there isn't currently a waiting list. It's an option.

On our way into town afterwards, we heard roars coming from Winchester College. The gates were open and we watched the last 15 minutes of what we later found to be Winchester football. This is a mixture of football and rugby and is played with a football on a long narrow pitch, the aim being to kick the ball over the opponent's line. Essentially a kick and charge game, the main skill is to kick straight. You can check out the rules if you like and you'll find terms such as tag, worms and handiwork, but it's a variant of what you and your mates would come up with given a football and a long afternoon. The game dates back to the sixteenth century and was first played by the students along Kingsgate Street, soon moving to the top of St Catherine's hill. A tradition built, which continues to this day. Only Winchester College play the game now, but in 1861 a schoolmaster introduced it to South Africa where it became the dominant code until 1878 when rugby union took over. Culture done, we headed for the pub.

The other incidents followed a similar pattern. He tracked through the *Chronicle* to find the theft of the Sparsholt mosaic from the top floor of the City Museum. Week twenty-two of the blog described the excellent City Museum, complete with replica nineteenth-century Winchester shops on the ground floor, Anglo Saxon Middle Ages on the first floor, and Roman Winchester on the second—including the fourth-century mosaic from the Sparsholt villa.

Dean Garnier Garden was breached next, the sleeping dog sculpture snatched—which Rob thought looked more like a fox. This corresponded with week forty-three's entry on the Cathedral Close area, including the garden—originally created as a rose garden by Dean Garnier around 1850, before being redesigned and reopened in 1995.

The attempt to steal the Town Clock on Lloyds Bank represented the only documented failure. Sure enough the blog spoke about this in week thirty-two, also mentioning the curfew bell that sits in a turret above the clock and is rung at 8:00 p.m. every evening—and has done for nearly nine hundred years, originally as a warning to extinguish home fires after a disastrous city fire.

Finally, the theft of the Round Table from the Great Hall provided the most recent incident. And there it was, week forty-one: Winchester Castle, and the Great Hall and Round Table. Rob skimmed the entry. The castle was built in 1067 and ordered to be destroyed by Oliver Cromwell in 1646. All that's left now is an excavation showing the remains of the round tower and the old city wall, part of the castle cellar…and the terrific Great Hall. The fourteenth-century Round Table on the wall depicts King Arthur at the centre with the names of his 24 knights around the edge. Sadly, Camelot, Sir Lancelot, Guinevere, Merlin, et al is but a legend, first made famous in Sir Thomas Malory's Le Morte d'Arthur of 1485.

Rob appreciated the coincidences but what else could they be? Someone reading his Year of Culture—unlikely in itself—and targeting each instalment? He had covered much of Winchester's culture in his blog, so if someone targeted known landmarks—for whatever reason—they'd naturally overlap with the blog.

He moved to the kitchen to prepare supper. A TV dinner in front of Doctor Who would round off the weekend. The salmon took a while to grill and he paced the flat, pausing at the PC as a thought occurred. The *Hampshire Chronicle* focused on Winchester and central Hampshire. The weekly culture had strayed from this area every third week or so—sometimes to Southampton, as with the City Gallery, and a few times to London. Scotland, Paris and Plymouth had also put in appearances. Any incident involving these locations wouldn't appear in the *Chronicle*, so would need a wider internet search.

Rob typed a query for thefts from the City Gallery. The first result was from the BBC Hampshire site and a number of others had the same headline: "£20,000 painting stolen from Southampton gallery." He read the text, picking out the key facts. "Break-in on night of 19 February…stolen painting had been on display but recently moved to basement store room…thief searched hundreds of pictures, ignoring more valuable ones…two witnesses saw masked man sprinting from building…painting under his arm…George Shaw's The Unicorn."

Rob let out a slow breath. He had a problem.

Chapter 9

A crowded Winchester train station, 6:27 Tuesday morning. Early May sunshine angled low over the opposite platform and almost banished the chill. Queues formed at uniform intervals along the platform. How did they know where the train would stop and where the doors would be? Regardless, Marianne bought a coffee and joined one of the queues. She heard her name called. A man pushed himself off the back wall and moved to meet her, coffee, newspaper and sandwiches in hand, laptop over his shoulder.

"Hi Marianne. You need the coffee at this time, don't you?" He touched her on the back, about the best greeting he could manage in his overloaded state.

A short pause and then "Hello Paul. How are you?"

"Trying to wake up. I've got a client meeting in London, hoping to get our first big deal."

"Good luck. I'm going to Oxford. An appointment with my project sponsor."

"Is that work-related—biochemistry if I remember? You're looking very chic."

"Well…professional but earnest, I think." She smoothed her jacket. "Actually no, it's a private project—exciting, but I can't tell you about it. Er, how's Rob?"

An announcement sounded for the approaching train.

"Rob's doing well," Paul said. "Shame things didn't work out with you two, but he's keeping busy. There have been a few…changes. Playing lots of tennis. He's even entered the Hampshire Cup."

"I do feel a bit sad—like you say, we didn't quite work out, but I hope we can be friends." The train stopped, the queue perfectly in line with the carriage doors. "You said changes?"

"Yes, fitness-related. My train's another few minutes yet."

Marianne stepped on her train and twisted back towards the platform. "What kind of changes, how extensive?"

The doors were sliding shut and Paul gave a wave.

*****

Marianne settled into a seat. The Hampshire Cup? He'd get massacred. Roger was going to win that anyway. And why hadn't Rob returned her texts? Or Roger, for that matter.

She pulled out her phone and opened the file on Project Hermes. All the familiar details flooded through her and she soon de-stressed, her mind revisiting the discoveries made and embracing the work to come. Although named after a Greek God with the abilities of extreme speed, flight, and a trickster's mentality, the project's aim hadn't been to explore any form of enhanced powers—at first. Marianne simply liked him: mostly benevolent and on humanity's side, mercurial, bold, and with the morals and mindset to see a mission through.

Her project was extracurricular research that made her feel at the cutting edge. She had always been the brightest at school, working moderately hard to come top in most subjects and especially the sciences. This led to a place reading biochemistry at London Imperial, one of the top universities for the subject…where she had a shock. Talent converged from all over the country and intimidated her. There were people smarter, quicker, better-read. She was still good, but only mid-stream. After a year of unmotivated underperformance, she compensated by hard work—a trait now bound into her character. She did well and gained a 2.1: not quite well enough for a top research post but enough to land a hard-fought job in food processing with a national dairy company. Again she was hard working, successful and made a difference…but something seemed to be missing. Hence the side project.

The molecular mechanisms of inflammatory disease had been her final year project, though she'd only scratched the surface. She resurrected and took it further by reading research journals, attending conferences and lectures and, after a while, getting permission to borrow work labs for private experiments. This kept her abreast of current research, but still searching for an individual angle or voice. She found it when considering ways in which the body can become "supercharged". There are a number of substances which can lead to superior cellular repair and growth. One example is anabolic steroids—valuable in treating certain diseases, but more commonly associated with drug cheats and dangerous side effects. More anecdotal tales of temporary super strength exist, the stock example being people lifting cars to rescue friends or family. A surge of adrenalin to the muscles is the generally accepted explanation, although difficult to test—and again, too much adrenalin persisting in the body is a danger to health. Street drugs such as "angel dust" have also been linked with superhuman strength, although possibly an urban myth. Marianne researched both the known and tenuous examples to try and understand the various mechanisms involved; then she looked at how they might be amalgamated and adapted to boost repair without major side effects.

She tried a few avenues, published some papers in an obscure journal, nothing earth-shattering. And then something happened. An unexpected result she couldn't explain, but a sketchy idea as to how to investigate. A further paper followed with some fairly wild and tenuous speculation. Next day, Professor Mark Wolf from Oxford got in touch. Brilliant, charismatic, an international name…Marianne was awestruck. He offered guidance, a small allowance, and weekend use of a futuristic lab. The only condition was for the work to remain secret until they were ready to publish. She accepted.

Fifteen months later and the project's direction had subtly changed. The important point was to achieve the greater good, to save people, and the main focus still to bolster the body's repair mechanism against disease and injury. But drug trials and certification wind a slow path, and an interesting offshoot emerged. A way to augment physical capabilities appeared tantalisingly close. Superpowers would be an exaggeration, but a thrilling idea. So many problems and so much evil in the world—if she had the power to challenge injustice where it was found….

The train pulled into Oxford and her third meeting with Professor Wolf approached.

*****

Twenty minutes to leave the station, cross Castle Mill Stream on Hythe Bridge Street, walk up the appropriately named Broad Street, left at the end and then right to the University Science Area, the whole route breathing history, academia and vitality. The New Biochemistry Building stood off South Parks Road, a stunning and transparent modern building with multi-coloured glass fins. Three flights of stairs and a narrow passageway led her to a reception room. Geoff, the professor's PA, asked her to wait in the office to the right and offered her a Rich Tea biscuit. She took it and walked in.

A display case to the left of the door housed a broad-bladed ceremonial sword. She moved towards an aged-looking leather armchair by a small table. She stood a while, perusing the room. A globe on the table showed the world sometime in the 1800s. A large mahogany desk faced her, a high-backed chair behind. Ten textbooks lay on the desk, five of them open at various points, extending in a rough diagonal line from a desktop computer. Oak bookshelves lined two of the walls and housed technical books in no obvious order, but well-thumbed enough to suggest the professor knew where everything was. Two lower shelves were set aside for non-science titles— Ancient Greece, science fiction anthologies and sword fighting intriguingly prominent. A grandfather clock stood in the corner to her front right—reproduction or original she couldn't tell—and an antique cabinet against the wall to her left. In an ultra-modern building, the office had fought back and projected an aura of age. Just needed a suit of armour.

Five minutes passed and Marianne sat down. The clock ticks started to become dominant. A creak sounded to her left. A second door, leading from the lab, opened and closed; with a swift stride he was upon her. Tall, light brown hair with enough length to be tousled, a day's stubble, open necked shirt and jacket. About forty. "Marianne. Welcome. I trust your journey was agreeable." A firm handshake and a hand on her shoulder. "Don't you want your Rich Tea? Geoff stocks them specially." A smile. "We have work to do."

"Hello Professor…Mark."

"Your last two reports were excellent. Clear, succinct, and progressing towards our end." He ushered her towards the lab, the biscuit dropped on the desk in passing. "I like the informal commentary you add, but you've held back lately. You're best letting your imagination flow, reach those wilder shores. When you think at the edge of what might, what could be happening, that's when you maximise creativity and work at a higher level."

"Yes, I understand." The lab was busy. Scientists hunched over chemical analysers or microscopes or computers, a man with a goatee beard appeared to be mixing chemicals under a fume hood, an earnest discussion took place at the end of an aisle. "I think I have two modes of working. I'll speculate and be bold—much more than I used to—ahead of each project phase. But once a section of research is defined, I'll go through the steps as planned, without deviating."

The professor stopped in front of a computer at the end of the far bench, a quiet enough area to be private. To their left, a row of DNA sequencers took up the rest of the bench. Floor to ceiling windows formed the external wall on their right. Just behind them a whiteboard attached to the back wall, filled with a scrawl of symbols and equations.

"Which is good scientific method, but you need something extra. To reach full potential—and especially for you, the way your mind sees patterns—you need to keep that creative thought alive every step of the way." One hand in his pocket and casual, he looked directly in her eyes. "And you have to tell me about it. We're close to something groundbreaking here. I need your insight to close this."

A single step, followed by a leap and a half turn placed him at the whiteboard, one arm outstretched towards her. "Take the section in your report on MAPK activation in macrophages. We're trying to control this to suppress destructive inflammation. We do need the activation as an immunity response, but we want to take it further and safely exploit the effect it has to boost healthy cells. Your report does suggest avenues of investigation." He erased the contents of the whiteboard and started scribbling. "But when you look at some of the other work we've done, like this or this"—he pointed at sections on the board—"there are further synergies. What if we could start from a normal state and safely encourage these cells, in combination with this inhibitory mechanism and this compensation here"—more pointing at the board—"to attack every piece of fatigue, every inefficiency in the body."

She thought a moment before replying, speaking in measured tone. "Disease resistance would show a major increase. The body would self-mend before you noticed any problems—no way to beat all pathogens of course, but even so. And the side effects…incredible fitness, the body would mop up waste products far quicker than normal, muscles would be at peak efficiency."

"Exactly."

"We're almost getting into sci-fi. This is the equivalent of nanobots running round the body fixing everything up…. That may happen one day, but not for a long time."

"That's the prize, Marianne." The professor put both hands on the bench and leaned towards her. "An effect that size may be unlikely, but partway is still going to create powerful waves."

Marianne saw something beyond the professor's usual authoritative and high-energy enthusiasm, so effective at engaging and challenging people—assuming you could keep up. An extra zeal stood out, as if this mattered more, at times overcoming his easy-going charm and creating an unpredictable manner. It unnerved her a bit, but her academic interest stayed to the fore and she pushed back.

"But it's not possible." She picked up a second marker pen and started to write. "Even if we introduced a mechanism into the body and avoided all these defences"—her turn to point at the board and trace connections—"and prevent any retaliatory reactions, we'd create a feedback loop. The process would become runaway. The patient would be harmed. Unless…at best there'd be a time limit before it stopped working, maybe only a matter of seconds."

The professor took over the board and they worked through scenarios and hypotheses. After a full eighty minutes they'd covered almost every angle of the project. Marianne necessarily held a narrow focus on the goal at hand because she lacked the breadth of subject commanded by the professor, who introduced ideas not only from other strands of biochemistry but from physics, medicine and even artificial intelligence. He pushed back three appointments with charm and promises to buy lunch or coffee, before switching his phone off.

Marianne asked for an update on the testing. Her work had focussed on theory and computer modelling. However, the use of the lab had advanced her skills to the point where she created some of the test samples. She didn't perform the actual testing—a PhD student of the professor's did this work. The standard way of introducing the modifications they were trialling was by injecting a virus (modified to remove its harmful effects) as a vector to carry additional material and insert it into target cells. Techniques to do this orally, by taking a pill, were feasible, but in their infancy, and they'd usually used injections. The PhD student, Julie, used mice from the biomedical department as test subjects. In broad summary, the mice didn't suffer harmful effects and there were modest but significant improvements in physical stamina.

Time ran out. The professor could delay his diary no longer and he summed up, reiterating the research to be done, ending with, "We're close, Marianne. There's a route to something great that must be possible. I have a key conference in September and I'd like significant progress by then, enough to announce results."

He rapped the desk and, for a second time, fixed her with a stare. "Make sure you send me all your hypotheses, anything might lead us to the final piece we need." Again, his manner became…not menacing, but overintense. He reverted to normal with a wide smile, and shook her hand, his other hand placed on her shoulder. "This has been a pleasure and your work is first-rate, Marianne. I look forward to our next meeting."

She left the lab, went through the office and into the reception room. Geoff was on the telephone. He said goodbye, not resuming his conversation until she left the room.

Marianne reversed her journey through the building and back to the station, deep in thought. She knew how to break through the problems they faced. It still led to obstacles she couldn't see past, but the research path seemed clear. The information was all there in her reports, in the brainstorming on the board, in their work over the last year. It just needed to be pieced together. And today, for the first time, she realised the professor hadn't done that. She was ahead of him. She wondered why she'd kept that from him.

Chapter 10

"I know it sounds crazy and he's a nice guy. But…."

The date had advanced to mid-May. Paul and Kate were enjoying early evening sunshine at a pavement table outside Greens Wine Bar. A lively atmosphere reigned amongst the after-work crowd. Several other groups sat or stood near them, and, inside, the long and narrow bar area was filling up. Rob had invited them to his flat for seven o'clock, projecting an air of mystery. They had half an hour to kill.

"Yes?" Paul said.

"He put a lot of effort into his Year of Culture—have you read the blog by the way?"

"About half."

"It's difficult to tell how seriously he treats it. He writes in a flippant manner like 'do I have to do this?', but then becomes drawn in and full of praise for bands or artists or historic monuments or…any kind of culture."

"Rob doesn't really know what he wants to do. I met him when we both started at the same electronics company, ten years ago. I moved on after a couple of years. He's still there, although, fair play, he has moved up to do a responsible job. He puts the effort in and stays late to hit deadlines, but you can see it's not his dream and there's no real focus or plan for a change. Similarly with the blog, he made the effort but didn't seem to treat it seriously, maintaining a…diffidence or tongue-in-cheek attitude."

"Yes—the importance or how much he cares is played down," Kate said. "Is that modesty? Lack of confidence?"

"A bit of both perhaps. The end result was good though.

He championed culture in his own way and dragged friends to events they wouldn't have seen otherwise." He paused. "You mentioned a 'but' earlier."

"Well." Kate sipped her wine. She folded her arms. "Someone's going around stealing the items Rob's written about. Seemingly someone with powers of great speed and strength and maybe even flight." She moved one hand up to her chin. "And Rob has these powers. Could he be…the Velvet Vandal?"

Paul laughed, shook his head.

"Perhaps without his conscious knowledge—some kind of Jekyll and Hyde effect."

"It's a plausible theory." Paul drained his remaining wine. "Rob can't be the Velvet Vandal. He simply isn't that type of person. The way he's acting is the way Rob would act if he suddenly got special powers. He's not sure what to do with them, so he's picked on something which he'll stick with—in this case, the tennis tournament. His conversation, his hopes and uncertainties are the same as ever."

"O…k," she said, with some hesitation. "I guess I don't know him like you. I just can't see any rational explanation. Rob develops impossible powers and, at the same time, a supervillain stalks Winchester stealing art or monuments described in a culture blog Rob wrote last year, which hardly anyone's read. And Rob's main focus is to win a tennis tournament. No novelist would write this."

"I don't understand either, but I think we play it straight. You know when you watch a TV show and everything's normal except one thing, like time travel or aliens loose in the city—"

"A talking horse?"

"Exactly. Of course you need to be sceptical. Once the situation is clear-cut, though, I think accepting it—like they do on TV—is the most practical thing to do. Then you can take advantage, enjoy the adventure. I'm sure that's what Rob's doing or he'd be more freaked out."

"I guess so," Kate said. "This must be possible, we just don't know how." She finished her drink, then opened and closed her mouth, hesitated. "I keep feeling there's something else, a picture beyond Rob and the culture. It's difficult to explain…a sensation at the edge of my mind."

"Could well be, Kate. This is pretty weird. Meantime, I think we help Rob and try and work out what's happening."

"Agreed. I can measure how his body performs. Finding the reason is much more difficult. I should really be talking with medical specialists about this—the situation is so unusual and I don't want to be responsible for not highlighting a health issue. I understand why Rob wants to keep things quiet, though."

"Understood," Paul said. "I think you're doing the best you can. There's nothing actually wrong with Rob and it is his decision." He gave her a smile. "There is a researcher we can talk to, someone closer to home—although it might be sensitive."

"Marianne?"

"Yee…s." Paul checked his watch. "Time to discover Rob's surprise."

They stood, dodged past a group of drinkers catching the sun, glanced at the million pound-plus houses in the estate agent's window on the right, crossed the High Street and started walking up Southgate Street towards St Cross.

When they reached the cinema, Kate said, "When you say

Rob is uncertain what he wants to do with himself and his powers, how about you?"

"I don't have any superpowers."

"There's always your dress sense."

Paul looked at his orange board shorts and overlarge, green polo shirt. Kate wore sports trainers, jeans and sleeveless black top. A double leather bracelet—blue—wrapped round her right wrist.

"Hey," he said. "To answer your deep question…. Since starting the business with Ravi, I've felt this is what I'm meant to do. Creating and growing a business motivates me more than any other job, especially after twelve years of engineering sales and ever-growing bureaucracy."

"So you're enjoying it?"

"Definitely. Lots of start-ups fail, though. We do need a break and a decent-sized order. Luckily, Ravi is an excellent programmer and quite visionary, so we have a shot at this." They turned right at the vets on the corner of Ranelagh Road. "On the personal side, things are going fine with Sarah and Liam. I feel a responsibility towards them, even if Sarah's far more organised and competent than me. I'm starting to think I should have a plan, or at least a paying job."

"Prospects?" Kate said.

Paul laughed. "I guess so. I don't think we're…I'm ready for marriage yet. But the business and personal life are connected." He turned towards her. "We're almost there and you haven't answered your own question."

"Doing the career I want" she said. "All patients are different and I find it such an interesting challenge working out what's wrong and fixing them. Sometimes frustrating, but I feel I'm innovating and making a difference. I think it helps that I settled on it fairly late, starting the physio degree at twenty-three." She paused. "Personal goals? I'd like to run a marathon…more travel…romance…." They arrived and she waved to Rob.

Good grief," Paul said.

Rob nodded to them. Before they could talk, he shook hands with a smart trouser-suited lady of about sixty and shepherded her to a car outside his drive. He opened the door and parted with a smile and a "Goodbye Mrs Jones, we'll be in touch presently."

Rob wore a forties-style suit, complete with waistcoat and navy cotton tie. A trilby rested on top of the garden wall a few yards away. Remnants of building materials were stacked against the wall in front of his garage—a few bricks, a bag of cement, some wood. The garage's full-width canopy door had been removed and replaced with a standard-sized dark green door, and the extra space had been bricked up. Frosted glass formed the upper half of the door. Lettering etched across two rows read Rob Griffin Detective Services.

"So you went for the detective idea," Kate said.

"Take a look," Rob said, stepping towards the garage. He picked up the trilby on the way.

The inside had been kitted out to form a basic office. A desk, bare apart from notepad and pen, stood close to the back wall. A chair behind it and a faded sofa in front created the setting for client discussions. A carpet covered the floor, and a filing cabinet in the corner and a whiteboard attached to the left wall completed the fixtures. Rob's bike rested against the right wall.

Kate nodded. "Stylish."

"Which bit?" Paul said.

"Well…Rob is."

"Thanks," Rob said. "Nice bracelet, by the way." She smiled.

"Rob—what on earth...?" Paul said. "Why are you creating a Philip Marlowe-type detective agency in your garage? And who's Mrs Jones?

Rob put the trilby on and adjusted the angle, placed his hands in his pockets and leaned against the back of the sofa. "No one tried to stop me," he said. "Mrs Jones is my client, came off the street with an interesting proposition."

"Um—"

"Didn't seem polite to turn her down."

"A big jewel heist?" Kate said.

Rob laughed. "No, someone chopped down the tree outside her garden wall. You might be wondering what this is about?"

"Well…." Paul said.

Rob re-adjusted his hat. "I think when you're unsure what to do, you have to pick something. Yes, there's the Hampshire Cup, but it doesn't take all my time and doesn't help people. Plus my job satisfaction is heading downwards. I'm product manager for the QT200. Do you know what a QT200 is?"

"Death ray?"

"Hair dryer?"

"Exactly. It actually provides testing for DSL and higher layers in telecoms circuits. If I didn't do it, I'd probably be product manager for something else you've never heard of."

"Someone has to do it, Rob," Kate said, "and I'm sure you do a good job."

"Well yes. But when you consider the superpowers, and that they should be used constructively, and that the tennis is just a diversion, and I've been doing my job too long, and deep down everyone wants to be a detective—don't they?—and sometimes you should do something bold…this is what happens." A sweep of his arms indicated the garage.

"You haven't quit your job?" Paul said.

"No. This is a test, a chance to assess the feasibility. I've adjusted my work hours to free up time for the detecting."

"How did you find Mrs Jones?"

"From the lady whose cat we saved, Cynthia. After the story ended up in this week's paper—"

"Ah yes," Paul said. Their photo and a short article headed "Cat rescued by mysterious 'Culture Man' " had appeared on page nine of the *Hampshire Chronicle*.

"I went to see her, said I knew Culture Man and asked how the cat was. She knows a few people like Mrs Jones with minor irritations, and she put the word out. She may suspect I'm Culture Man, I'm not sure, but she's nice and we have an understanding."

"Wow," Kate said. "That could be a good client base."

"True," Rob said. "I'm calling it the silver market. These people are generally active, semi-retired, wealthy—used to hiring competent people. If I can get a foothold…." He paced a few steps. "Of course, I still need one client who's a glamourous international starlet. Anyway, I got my friend Phil to help with the changes to the garage. The suit is only for marketing, to make an impression at meetings. I'm not planning to prowl Winchester dressed like this."

"Fair enough," Paul said. "How about your nemesis, the Velvet Vandal?"

Rob moved to his left and pointed to the whiteboard on the wall, on which a central circle labelled "Winchester" had been drawn. Outlying circles were marked "Southampton", "Marwell Zoo", "Plymouth"…there were several others. Crosses also dotted the board, minuscule writing next to them.

"The red crosses show the culture that's been attacked, for example St Cross Hospital on 3 April." He pointed at the relevant area. "The green crosses are the entries from my cultural blog that haven't been hit, for example Marwell Zoo."

"Can you spot any obvious pattern?" Kate said.

"No. The incidents don't follow the chronological order of the blog and there isn't any geographic pattern."

"So can we work out what's next? Some must be more likely than others."

"True. I should be able to narrow it down. Not all my cultural events are practical targets: for example, a Status Quo concert last year—there's nothing to steal. I can try and work out the most likely target and either warn or stake them out."

"Be careful." Kate glanced round the office and at Rob's detective attire. "But this is brilliant, Rob. Whatever happens, you've made the effort and created an adventure."

Rob smiled. "Should be a busy summer. I need to hold down my job, win the tennis tournament, solve Mrs Jones' case, establish the detective business, and unmask the Velvet Vandal."

"Need any help?" Paul said.

"Thanks—I'll put you on speed dial."

Kate had to go. She was meeting Arnold—mostly so she could "prove him wrong on more or less everything."

Rob scanned his office and studied the whiteboard again. "I didn't think she liked him," he said.

"Quick pint down the Queen?"

"Sure."

Chapter 11

Anteater stolen: Velvet Vandal strikes again

No longer can we be shocked. A line has been crossed. First a lesson on anteaters, and then the shock. There are four types of anteaters, all native to South and Central America. You have probably never heard of the silky anteater—this is the miniature tree-living version, only a foot long including the tail. Next come the northern tamandua and the southern tamandua, both about four foot long with distinctive black stripes and difficult to tell apart; equally at home in the trees or on the ground. None of these are endangered, though the tamanduas may be captured as pets. Now the giant anteater. A noble animal: a six-foot ground dweller; powerful but shy; eating up to thirty thousand ants or termites a day; a good swimmer using—believe it or not—the front crawl; hunted by jaguars but capable of fighting back. The Red List of Threatened Species classifies it as vulnerable.

Marwell Zoo is proud to host a breeding pair and the first young anteater, Hector, was born last year. Now be shocked. Hector is gone. Not escaped like a teenage rebel with the wrong crowd. Stolen. Closing time drew near when a harsh medley of noise startled June Ainsley as she walked past the anteater enclosure. There was a deep tuba-like roar and a high pitched squealing, followed by a metallic crash and a loud shout. Looking back, she saw a figure perched on top of the enclosure fence, struggling to hold a squirming sack. The light was grey and the only features she could distinguish were a dark cloak and mask. In no time the figure had leapt down and streaked across the fields, leaving an adult anteater on hind legs banging her front claws against the cage.

Alison Townsend, the zookeeper, was upset and furious. "This is an awful crime," she said. "We're trying to save these animals. Hector will be very frightened. He's an eighteen-month-old juvenile not used to being without his mother. More importantly, the public will not know how to look after him. Anteaters in captivity need an expertly prepared diet—a special combination including fruit, eggs, milk and ground beef—or they may not eat. I appeal to anyone with information to tell us and help find Hector."

This time the Velvet Vandal goes too far. It is one thing to attack Winchester's heritage, even a game perhaps. But here a young life is at stake. That is why I say these crimes can no longer shock us and this must desist. As the police still search for the Round Table and now urgently seek our anteater, be assured I will continue to report and bring you the latest news.

Marianne didn't often read the *Hampshire Chronicle*. International affairs were her news of choice, world changing events and large-scale injustice highest on the radar. As a consequence she'd been unaware a masked villain stalked Winchester with a random list of cultural targets. Curiosity battled for her attention against a dim recognition of the byline: Jerome Laroche. Why was that name familiar? Presumably French, and Bordeaux stuck in her mind—she'd collaborated with Bordeaux University on and off, most recently visiting six months ago. But no…she couldn't place him.

Her gaze lifted from the paper and swept the café, which merged with the surrounding library. The library formed part of the Winchester Discovery Centre, an impressive modern building also containing an art gallery, an exhibition space upstairs, and an events hall used for lectures, comedy and the like. It was nine fifteen, the last Saturday in May, and Paul should arrive soon. She spotted him entering the side entrance near the cake display. Bookshelves and a group of students hid her, so she stood and waved.

Paul dodged past chairs and people to reach her table. He checked her coffee requirements and retreated to the café counter, returning with two lattes.

They swapped some quick news and then discussed tennis. Marianne had started playing in the team, helped by some coaching from Roger. She enjoyed it, quite a challenge—but so frustrating playing against experienced doubles partners. Quite often they weren't athletic, but had played together for years and knew just where to place the ball, stroking it back, standing in perfect position at the net until eventually you blast it out—aaargh! Paul had withdrawn from the team this year, busy with work and personal commitments, and also helping Rob with the Hampshire Cup—"Oh yes, and what's that about?"—which led to the subject of their meeting.

"Your texts about Rob have been quite guarded, Marianne."

"Yours too, Paul. Mysterious, even."

They continued the discussion upstairs in the exhibition room, expecting to find some privacy. It was a restful room where people drifted in and out through the day, but only two or three at a time. Photos from The Wildlife Photographer of the Year were on show. This displayed at London's Natural History Museum each year and a subset of the winning photos toured the country. Winchester took its turn through May. Two other people were in the room.

"Can you describe the changes you mentioned in Rob?" Marianne said.

"He's fitter these days."

"How much fitter?"

"A lot fitter. You said in your text, that you thought there could be a medical reason."

"How do you measure the changes? Have you checked gym work or running times? I could guess at a medical explanation, but it's confidential, I can't speak about that."

"His running times are classified."

"What?"

Paul studied the photograph facing them, which had won the black and white category of the competition. It showed Arctic terns against a stormy sky. They spend eight months on the wing, migrating from the Arctic to the Antarctic and back again—chasing eternal sunshine, Paul remembered Rob telling him.

He pointed at the photo. "The Wildlife Photographer of the Year was one of Rob's cultural events; he visited the Natural History Museum last year and wrote a blog entry." A pause. "Do you care about him?"

"Yes. I do." She gave a wistful smile and...kind of meant it. "Rob's intentions are good. He's enthusiastic, kind. His problem is he's drifting, and he has to solve that himself."

"Shall we make a pact? An honest exchange of information."

Marianne stared at him and hesitated for two, three seconds. She nodded, reached out her hand and they shook.

"He can run the hundred metres in six seconds," Paul said.

"He swallowed something from my lab that might produce superpowers."

They swapped stories. Paul didn't mention the flying. Marianne didn't mention Professor Wolf or her growing wariness of him, just an "illustrious sponsor".

Snippets of conversation passing back and forth included: "There's no way my samples could cause that effect", "You've been creating a superhero potion in your cellar?", "It's a spin-off, we're trying to understand disease mechanisms", "He puts it down to a lizard bite", "Who's Kate?", "I've no idea what kind of lizard", and "No, not dangerous, probably not anyway."

Marianne focused on the lizard. "Somehow the bite must have reacted and magnified the effect. I need more details. Can I speak to Rob?"

"He's playing the second round of the Hampshire Cup at ten thirty. You can catch him afterwards—at the Bereweeke Club."

"You're not watching?"

"No, I'm out for the day with Sarah and Liam. Rob's ready, though. He won the preliminary round 6-4 6-4, the first round 6-2 6-3, and we've made some improvements since. He is playing the second seed though."

"Tim Foster? Surely he doesn't stand a chance?"

"We'll see."

Marianne led the way out of the exhibition, both stopping for a final glance at the winning entry: a snow leopard prowling a strip of mountainside through gusting snow. The picture had been captured by camera trap due to the difficulty of photographing such a rare and remote animal. "There is one thing," she said. "I expect his powers to run out."

"Really? Any idea when?"

"Yes, we should be able to be quite precise. Let's see, six months minus a couple of weeks due to dispersal effects"— she checked the diary on her phone—"would put it around the fifth of September."

They agreed to update Rob on their discussion, but not to mention the time limit for now. Paul thought, that although Rob had taken them in his stride, he had embraced the powers and their loss would be a blow. Marianne said goodbye and left the building.

Paul pulled out his phone. Some emails needed attention and he scanned through them, helped by a second cup of coffee. He figured he should call Rob before the tennis match and before Marianne waylaid him, but decided to wait until he got home. Based on a sketchy recollection, he sent a quick text asking the date of the tennis final. The response came back shortly after he left the Discovery Centre: "5 September."

*****

Loss aversion. A tendency to prefer avoiding loss than acquiring gains. You find twenty pounds in the morning and lose twenty pounds in the afternoon: the loss hurts more than the gain pleases, you end up annoyed. Professional golfers sink par putts more frequently than birdie putts of the same length: every putt is important, but somehow they try harder to avoid dropping par. You do six great things for your partner and one annoying thing: guess which is remembered? You're playing the number two seed in the Hampshire Cup, you've done brilliantly, won the first set, went close in the second and the decider stands at 4-4: you can hold your head high, expectations are exceeded, and you don't absolutely have to win, do you? Alternatively, you're the second seed playing an also-ran, and it's unexpectedly tight, 4-4 in the decider: no way are you going to lose in the second round, your concentration stiffens, you pull out your top game—and usually win. All facets of loss aversion: keeping what you have and justifying expectations is more important than reaching for the sky.

It can be overcome. Boris Becker in his first Wimbledon final, 1985. Kevin Curren reached his peak, demolished John McEnroe and Jimmy Connors in the quarter- and semi-finals; only the eighth seed but firm favourite against unseeded seventeen-year-old Becker. Becker would not be beaten though. He was single-minded, diving headlong for volleys, stating he went on court to win, to fight. He ended up a deserved winner in four sets, the springboard to a career at the top, winning six Grand Slam titles and achieving the number one ranking.

Sometimes it's a one-off rather than a breakthrough to the top, one glorious moment. Juan Martin Del Potro in the US Open Final, 2009. Roger Federer at the height of his powers, winner of the last five US Opens, playing his twenty-first Grand Slam final—only Rafael Nadal had beaten him in such finals. Federer two sets to one up—and then Del Potro clicked. Massive forehands, massive nerves. The fourth set taken in a tie-break. The fifth set won convincingly in a devastating display of controlled power. Del Potro remained a top player but didn't consistently grace the upper echelon, partly due to multiple injuries. The 2009 US Open remains the pinnacle, although further glory could yet follow.

Rob had won the first set 6-2; fast movement, accurate length and a low error count surprising his opponent. The second set had stood 4-4. Rob had chances but Tim was strong—deep ground strokes, wide serves, good net positions, angled volleys. Rob's powers only gave so much advantage. When he fired a shot from one side and Tim put an acute volley to the other side, he couldn't reach it. Nor did he want to use ridiculous speed—from a practical point of view he ended up unbalanced and, in addition, there was a...fairness issue. Rob lost his serve from game point up to go 5-4 down, and Tim served out to level the match at one set all.

So, 4-4 in the final set and Rob serving at 0-30 down. Tim looked the stronger, shots well placed and consistent—accepting Rob would reach some unreachable shots and hit some winners, but knowing what to do. Determination and confidence solid. Rob had done his best, the score would be close, he could be proud: the wrong attitude.

Rob served and a rally progressed. He'd never won a sporting event. Twenty shots, twenty-five, a long rally. He concentrated on footwork and moving fast to the ball. A mistake from Tim, an angled stroke landing in the tramlines. 15-30. Three shots into the next rally and slightly short from Tim. Rob hit deep and moved in. Tim was taken by surprise on the backhand and hit into the net. 30-30 and the next point crucial. Tim gained the upper hand; he picked a short shot and moved to the net. Rob had choices, none easy: down the line, cross court or a lob. Don't get caught in two minds. He relaxed and went down the line, and yes! 40-30. Rob needed to fix his career, find a satisfactory purpose in life, a girlfriend, all kinds of half-ambitions in his mind…he also wanted something now, you could promise for ever. It was time to win. A deep breath, a hard serve and Tim returned long. 5-4 Rob.

Tim served to stay in the match. The first point would pile pressure on the loser and Rob stayed solid, Tim hitting long. 0-15. Tim lost discipline in the next, going for an improbable winner and missing. 0-30. A service winner pulled the score back to 15-30. Rob dug in on the next point, not giving anything and Tim blinked first. 15-40. Match point. A long rally, Rob determined to keep the ball deep. Tim deliberately dropped the ball short, pulled Rob into the net. A bold move and a rat-a-tat rally at the net followed, which could have gone either way. Rob lunged for a volley, Tim scooped a cross-court return, wrong-footing him, but Rob twisted back, reached out and flicked his wrist, angling a volley beyond Tim. It kissed the line and he'd won.

Tim showed true sportsmanship with a rueful smile, a long handshake and "A brilliant match, Rob. Well played and good luck for the rest of the tournament." Rob felt elated—and mentally drained. He headed for the showers, remembering Paul's phone call and that Marianne would likely be waiting outside.

Chapter 12

Marianne was sitting on the wall outside the reception area. She wore jeans and a casual grey sweatshirt top, dark hair tied in a ponytail. Rob hadn't seen her for a couple of months. Still five foot six and slim. Still the small nose, a sprinkling of freckles. Still attractive.

He raised his eyebrows. "Hi," he said.

She didn't swoon, but stood and embraced him instead. "Hi," she said. "Getting up to much?"

"Well, you know." He moved his rucksack from his shoulder and held it in his left hand. "Won my tennis match."

"You're kidding. That's amazing, Rob."

They walked around the grounds, paying half attention to a couple of games in progress. Rob talked her through his match. Marianne updated him on some gossip. Rob explained his job remained much the same but he did have an after-hours initiative with his, um, detective services. Marianne's job was uncharacteristically quiet, but ok, she also had a private project.

"A secret lab in your cellar?"

"A bit more complicated than that. I hear you're the fastest man on the planet."

"Possibly." They'd stopped beyond the far court, no longer watching the tennis. "I figured all the work I'd done made my muscles super-efficient and then I got some kind of neurological boost—based on the timing, the lizard bite being the realistic candidate."

"Not very likely is it?"

"No. But in a way, that doesn't matter. Whatever the reason, I've got these powers so all I can do is see how events play out."

Rob gave a demonstration. They stepped through a break in the hedge to find a patch of grassland. He borrowed eight coins from Marianne's purse and placed them in a circle, each six feet away from him at the centre. He lunged to pick them up, returning to the centre after each one. His movement was a blur and he handed Marianne back the coins after five seconds.

Marianne was visibly impressed. They moved back towards the courts, and she filled him in on her research—the same details she'd told Paul.

"You kept that quiet."

"Yes…sorry. It was confidential, and never intended as a study of superpowers. You swallowed the sample from the cellar? What were you thinking of?"

"Ah yes. A mix up with the jam in your kitchen." She opened her mouth, closed it again. "You had to be there."

"I think you could be right about the lizard. Nothing else makes sense, a freak reaction that amplified the effect. Can you give me details?" Some strands of hair had escaped the ponytail and she brushed them from her face.

"Er…green—or perhaps olive—and about a foot long. I got bitten on the right leg, back of the calf. It stung at first and bruised afterwards, and I felt completely wiped out for two days. A few days later, these powers appeared. Kate's taken a stack of measurements."

"Hmmm." She spoke reflectively, to herself more than to Rob: "I can find out the type of lizard, given the location. I need to rethink this, try and understand how this combination could have such an effect."

She asked him about the detective agency, wondering about

his motivation. She also questioned the ambition. "Winchester's safe. There must be areas where you can make a major difference, use these powers to combat real evil or deprivation?"

"You mean Romsey?"

Marianne sighed.

Rob agreed to her request for a blood sample. She said goodbye and walked back to her car. He watched until she rounded the corner and disappeared from sight. And for a bit longer.

He forced his attention onto the tennis, followed a few rallies. After a while, he remembered the latest incident in the *Hampshire Chronicle*. He pulled up the culture blog on his phone and scrolled down to week ten.

Week 10 (2 Mar-8 Mar): Marwell Zoo

My mum visited from Somerset for a few days this week. I needed a venture to both entertain her and tick off the weekly culture, and I'd left it to Sunday afternoon. But no problem—you can't go wrong with the zoo. Now let me moderate that statement before I move on. I can appreciate some controversy on the morality of zoos. First: Do they exploit nature and only seek to exist in terms of a commercial venture? Or is there a focus on the animals, are they given space and stimulation, is there an altruistic motive in the realms of conservation and education? Marwell Zoo, a few miles down the road from Winchester, is run by Marwell Wildlife, a charity, and I think passes this test. Founded in 1972, it was one of the first European zoos to place an emphasis on conservation; it's involved in many such projects and runs rare breeding programs including one for the critically endangered Amur leopards. Space-wise, I can't judge what's needed, but the animals roam safari-park enclosures rather than being confined to cages. Second and more philosophical, on the nature of freedom: if animals are well cared for, stimulated, live longer, are removed from the reach of predators— which all sounds pretty cushy to me—even granted this, are they somehow less free, have they lost something? I'll leave you to ponder this, but Marwell's heart is clearly in the right place and the zoo is well-run, educational and generally excellent.

Now onto the animals…first, though, a diversion on my mum. She lives on her own—which can be lonely and the fate of many people these days—but she's optimistic and finds the positives. She likes animals and talks to them, whether it be the robin in the garden or the daddy longlegs on the ceiling. She knows they don't think like us (or do they?) but she'll invent stories and motivations for them and put them in her letters. The point is, the animals that most engage her are those she can construct a story around.

Back to the zoo. The most impressive animals are the big cats, and especially the tigers. Their casual manner and languor contrasts with the visible power which you know could be turned on in a flash. The cheetahs, part of a high-profile conservation program, are sleeker than the tigers and their power is based on phenomenal speed as opposed to pure majesty. We can't leave the cats without mentioning the snow leopards, again part of a breeding program—stunning-looking and a privilege to see such rare animals. My mum liked the grazing animals, the antelopes catching her eye. They provide plenty of scope for a narrative, with a broad territory to explore, a natural curiosity and the awareness that predators are all around—even if they're (probably) safe. Also the owls! To be honest, they all deserve a mention, they're outside our normal experience and each have their own stories. Final word is reserved for the giant anteater, an extraordinary animal, which entertained us both—and eats, of course, fish and chips. A great afternoon all round!

Chapter 13

Summer swooped across the landscape. Winchester High Street basking and bustling, culture scattered along its length from the medieval gateway of the Westgate Museum at the top to King Alfred's towering statue at the bottom. The meadows of St Cross stretching Winchester to the edge of the wonderful South Downs: rolling hills, chalk ridges, working farmland and ancient woodland, all sprinkled with clear streams and scenic villages. The sweep of coastline to the south, from Poole to Chichester, begging to be explored. Long hot days delivering a sparkle and a zip. Long rainy days as well—this is the UK—but no matter, each day alive with the potential for adventure.

Life continued with the added stardust of the season. Lots of things happened, but somehow summer suspended change, nothing evolving. Marianne locked herself in research, a breakthrough tantalizingly close and Professor Wolf ever in the background—but still time to escape for an hour or two a day. Paul developed the software business whilst chasing their first major client. A week's holiday on the Welsh coast with Sarah and Liam provided time out. Kate juggled her practice and multi-disciplinary website with continued monitoring of her superhero client, a little internet dating on the side. Paul and Kate both found themselves dragged into Rob's detective service from time to time. Rob had a ball: he reduced work to standard hours, engaged in a sporadic search for his nemesis, advanced through the tennis draw and, most of all, pursued his detective dream. The Velvet Vandal seemed to take a holiday, just a few low-profile heritage items stolen. Somewhere in a closed-off patch of wasteland, sustained by regular food drops, an anteater snuffled through the undergrowth.

Yet the summer fools you, it winds down and you find that all along events were ticking towards a conclusion, a reckoning. A montage of episodes shows a flavour of the summer and, perhaps, the structure that was always there.

*****

Rob had no idea how to find out who chopped Mrs Jones' tree down. He figured that if he started in some way, he'd learn something and work out what to do next. He checked the tree stump. A smooth surface covered three-quarters of the cross section before turning to jagged splinters. The lower reaches of St Catherine's Hill supplied an abandoned branch for comparison. He sawed through it and snapped the final part, finding the same pattern.

The tree had been about twelve foot tall, providing extra privacy beyond the garden wall and also an assembly point for sparrows and a gymnastic squirrel. Mrs Jones pointed out a similar tree at the end of her road. Careful study of the *British Tree Guide* from the library told him it was a Norwegian Maple.

He spoke to the Council. They'd removed the fallen tree from the pavement. A replacement would be planted of about the same size but wasn't a priority. No similar incidents had been reported.

The house stood in a quiet residential area. He hung around after school closing and spoke to some of the kids who passed. They were polite and slightly boisterous, and yes, had noticed the fallen tree one morning, but knew nothing of the cause. Then one, John—about thirteen years old and with his friend Naomi—said, "There's another one chopped down, looks the same, at the start of the lane through there."

Rob followed his directions and ended up ten yards beyond a row of houses and facing a shrubbed area. A stump showed the same markings, this time the rest of the tree still attached by a few fibres and lying in the bushes behind. He was starting to get somewhere.

*****

Late night Radio 2 helped distract Marianne from a problem that wasn't going anywhere. Molecular models flicked across her laptop, trying to tell her how Rob's lizard bite might interact with the sample he'd eaten. There weren't many venomous lizards in the world and certainly none in the Greek Islands. Her best guess was that the reptile in question was a stellion lizard, but it didn't really help. She figured Rob's body had reacted to something in the saliva, and it was his body's own reaction that had boosted the effect and led to his extraordinary abilities.

A documentary on big band musicians became the dominant pull on her attention. She rose from the kitchen table and poured a glass of milk from the fridge. The interview drifted into the meanderings of her mind: her next tennis match, how she could use superpowers to do so much good, Roger's latest text…. And then she had it. Not the solution to her problem, but Jerome Laroche.

She'd met him on her second trip to Bordeaux. They'd stayed at the same guest house in the Capucins district. Long hours at the university meant they only crossed paths as she was coming and going, usually in a tired state. He'd been a mature student, studying journalism with a special interest in…she couldn't recall. She remembered his enthusiasm but not the details. He had offered to tell her more over dinner—unfortunately she ended up too busy to follow through. He had still been there on her next visit and again she didn't find time to catch up. A shame. Remembering now, he'd been friendly and interesting. She found his email address on the *Hampshire Chronicle* website, sent a quick hello and went to bed.

*****

The car proceeded along Worthy Lane and passed the elegant façade of the 1930s Lido at the corner of Hyde Church Lane. The swimming pool had long gone but a rich history remained: commandeered by the military during the war and subsequently a dance hall hosting top bands including the Rolling Stones in 1963. A charity now ran the building as a community and sports centre. The car turned round and nosed into the car park opposite the Lido.

"Been on many stakeouts?" Paul said.

"First one. We should savour it."

"Remind me of the details."

"Mrs Deacon thinks her seventy-two-year-old husband is having an affair. He's suddenly started going out more, including—so he says—to yoga tonight. She wants me to follow him."

"Are you going to take her money for that?"

"No."

"Then why are we doing this?"

"It's a stakeout. Think Miami Vice, Starsky and Hutch, Midsomer Murders…hang on."

An older man of medium height approached the Lido

entrance. He wore trainers, tracksuit trousers and an overcoat, and walked with a slight stoop. Rob checked against a photo. "Yes that's him, eight o' clock as expected." He wrote into a notebook. "We need to wait for him to come out now."

"How long will that be, exactly?"

"If you include coffee and a chat, should be about ninety minutes."

*****

"Thank you so much for your help and seeing me so late."

Jennifer was effusive and Kate guided her out the door. "A pleasure. Remember you can call me with any questions and I'll see you in two weeks."

Kate typed some quick notes and shut the computer down. Ten years of back pain. Jennifer going from a confident thirty-eight-year-old working mum to someone…well, she remained positive, but even so, someone resigned to periodic pain, restricted lifestyle, less joy in her life. Discomfort in the lower back and left hip the prime symptoms, controlled by painkillers; flare-ups incapacitating her and causing missed work and family occasions.

She'd taken advice and treatment from a series of professionals—walking helped and certain exercises made a difference. But it all took time and money and she eventually settled, managing the condition as best she could.

Kate felt despair and anger—ten years! Not that anyone was necessarily culpable, but Jennifer's life had been reduced and dominated by this. She had started to massage out trigger points in the glutes and spinal muscles. She would also set up an online exercise plan which Jennifer could fill in and Kate add comments to, showing someone cared. She didn't know the best and most efficient answer, though. This was exactly why she'd kicked off her local multi-disciplinary group—to track down the best and most practical treatment for patients like Jennifer. The group met once a week to discuss each other's tougher cases, and review updates to the website.

Kate locked up. She was due to meet Arnold in town in forty minutes. She didn't think of it as a date, more a distraction. Arnold would question her and hold forth on the answers to pretty much everything and explain his strategy to reach the top. She'd sometimes challenge, sometimes let him flow. But he was intelligent and confident, and some of his advice would be good. Maybe it was a date.

*****

"How long's gone now?"

"Fifteen minutes," Rob said.

Paul sighed. "I'll send Sarah a text. She's acting a bit off lately: nothing obvious, says everything's fine but…less time, less enthusiasm for anything."

"Hmmm. Kate's seeing Arnold tonight. He invited her to a jazz thing at the Guildhall. Can you believe she turned down this stakeout for that?"

"Incredible."

Silence for a while. "Why don't you take Sarah and her son on holiday?" Rob said. "Maybe she's stressed."

"That…may be one of your better ideas."

Some more silence and then Rob returned to Kate. "I'm not sure she really likes Arnold. She says he acts like the ultimate solution to anything will come from him. Meanwhile

I'm a superhero, modestly doing my stuff."

"Have you made any kind of move?"

"No." He paused. "It's tricky. We get on well and see each other anyway because of the superpowers. Something needs to happen to…change the dynamic. I can't just dive in or it'll end a disaster, awkward at least."

"Just relax, Rob. Enjoy the friendship—and who knows."

Rob played with the radio tuner, settling on Radio Solent: the pick of music from the 1950s and '60s. They knew all about Motown by the time Mr Deacon came out at nine twenty-five.

Their surveillance target leapt down the Lido steps two at a time. He performed a couple of lunges before standing up straight. Three inches had been added to his height, putting him close to six foot. A group emerged at the top of the steps. A woman—probably the teacher—appeared to be offering all-round encouragement, before breaking away and joining the man. She was fortyish, slim and taut with short dark hair, a touch of curl. They chatted and laughed for a couple of minutes. She touched his arm gently and he was on his way.

"I should take up yoga," Paul said.

Rob waited a few minutes and then drove along Mr Deacon's homeward route, stopping occasionally and keeping him in sight. The stoop reappeared as he neared home.

*****

Marianne thought she saw how it could be done. Her analysis showed three mechanisms potentially leading to a massive muscular boost. They'd manifest in different ways; the most likely being a temporary effect of about six months, which is what she suspected had happened with Rob. The alternatives were a yoyo effect—powers waxing and waning in unpredictable fashion—and a permanent, or at least long-term, change.

She'd done her best to synthesize a product that she thought would provoke a similar reaction to the lizard bite. Combining this with her existing samples and adding a few refinements should give a chance of creating the drug they sought. However, none of the possibilities were likely. And even if she got lucky, the process was chaotic—a tiny variation, perhaps a slight difference in impurities, and the effect would disappear. It would be possible to create the drug and never be able to repeat the procedure.

She booked time in the Oxford lab to give it a go, managing to reserve the whole of next weekend. Her report to Professor Wolf could wait until afterwards despite his emails, mainly because university business had called him to Japan.

*****

The summit of Old Winchester Hill on the South Downs at 6:00 a.m. Kate had driven Rob towards East Meon before work—the sun warm enough for the top to be down on her Hyundai Coupe. They'd hiked to the top, finding the place deserted. An Iron Age hill fort and Bronze Age burial mounds betrayed themselves by the contours of the ground, and also by signs pointing them out. The soft light—a hint of red remaining from sunrise—illuminated a far-reaching landscape: patchwork fields, woodlands, meadowland and isolated trees melding together to produce a unique scene. The South Downs are not that high, but the relative flatness of the surrounding countryside makes for magnificent ridge views.

She watched him streak across the sky, fifty feet above her. Slowing and turning, the motion switched to bold swoops, one after another to barely ten feet, separated by sharp climbs. Attaining one peak, he stalled, appearing motionless for one…two…three seconds prior to embarking on a deep parabola-shaped dive. This time he almost brushed the ground before soaring back to his original height. Another couple of minutes in the air—twisting, turning, loops, displays of speed—continued to demonstrate sheer freedom and joy. He returned to earth at a shallow angle and landed two-footed, next to her.

Kate didn't say anything for a moment. She turned to face him and said, "That's absolutely stunning."

"I've been practising," Rob said.

*****

Roger. Five years older than her at forty-one. Polite and a dry sense of humour. Five times Hampshire Cup champion. Married briefly in his twenties, though he never talked about it. Worked as an accountant, often based in London. Hugely respected. Looked a bit nervous today.

He'd just partnered Marianne to a narrow win against a skilful tennis pairing. They walked across the sports centre carpark to Roger's car.

She nudged him. "I've never seen you like that, when you lost your serve. You were angry."

"No I wasn't." He put his kit in the car, kept a straight face for a moment, and then smiled. "All right, I admit it. Angry with myself—three volleys on the trot missed."

She lived close by so would walk back, but lingered.

"Roger."

"Marianne."

"Have you checked if you're free for the music festival? It would be nice to get together away from the area. Or maybe something else—there's the weekend walking I mentioned."

"Sorry—I can't make the festival, family stuff. I'm quite busy, but…yes…the walking should be fine. This is a…busy year for me, lots of priorities. Marianne, I wouldn't expect too much from this…but yes…I'm sure we can…manage something."

"Oh."

They stayed a minute or so. A further tennis session was agreed, although no date set. Marianne walked home.

*****

Rob tidied up his notes in the converted garage. A sense of tradition stopped him transcribing them to a laptop. Instead, he filed them in separate folders in the filing cabinet. He had four cases now: as well as Mrs Jones and Mrs Deacon, there was a missing cat and a stolen bicycle. He studied the whiteboard, updated to show the Velvet Vandal's latest activity. He had spoken to some of the witnesses, without gaining any more clues than the papers gave. A knock sounded on the door. A woman entered before he could respond.

"You're the detective?" she said.

She looked at least thirty years younger than his other clients. She wore heeled ankle boots, jeans and simple white blouse, undone enough to show a gold necklace. Midnight-black hair flowed over her shoulders, slender eyebrows overlooked light grey eyes, red lipstick…she was beautiful.

"I said—"

"Yes, I am."

"Good. I'm Natalie. The lady at my church spoke of you—Mrs Jones."

An accent filtered through the clear English. Rob wasn't good at accents and couldn't place it. "What can I help you with?"

"To solve a murder."

"A murder?"

"Yes. You can handle that?"

*****

The shadows lengthened outside the biochemistry building. Only a couple of bikes remained in the racks and no one had crossed the square for ten minutes. Eight o'clock on Saturday evening and Marianne's third straight weekend in the lab. She stared out the window, finished for the day. Thomas, the only other person in the lab, tapped on a computer at the opposite end of her bench. She should be on the train home by now, but Professor Wolf—returning from his travels that day—wanted to speak to her. He was late.

Her rucksack contained two samples, buried at the bottom. She had run a complex synthesization, which included many chemical reactions, and had repeated the process nigh on a hundred times. Each time, she altered the parameters slightly, but this wasn't her area of expertise and likely her technique added random changes. Nevertheless, microscopic analysis suggested two of the runs may have hit gold: one each of the permanent and temporary solutions predicted by her research. She had provided small amounts of each for Julie to test, with the tacit agreement not to tell the professor yet.

A detailed report existed on her laptop. Minor revisions and final test results were needed to complete it. She'd sent the professor an interim report, with much missed out, earlier in the week.

Marianne sensed the end of the project approaching. She was close to following her research to a logical conclusion, roughly in line with Professor Wolf's deadlines. Success—stunning success—seemed at hand, albeit in an unpredictable manner. She should feel excitement and elation as the finish line came in sight, banishing memory of the long slog, the setbacks, the midnight hours…but this time anxiety and uncertainty ruled. Despite the professor's assertion that they would announce initial results and then sit down to plan follow-up work, it struck her as vague. She didn't know how the research would be used or followed up or if she would be involved further.

The professor's erratic behaviour lay at the root of her concerns. Sometimes as dazzling as he'd always been and treating her as an equally brilliant confidante; yet others, demanding and almost suspicious. She hadn't realised why at first, but, ironically, it was his own evasions and reduced collaboration that had led her to withhold parts of her research. She would have to provide full details with the final report though—wouldn't she?

Thomas said goodbye and left. She looked out the window again. A lone student unlocked one of the bikes and cycled away. A hand on her elbow and she jumped.

"We have a problem," Professor Wolf said. No smile.

*****

She was Welsh. And married, although her husband had disappeared. Her husband wasn't the murder victim; it was her friend Johanna, owner of an art gallery in Southampton.

The gist of it went like this: Johanna had been found dead at the foot of Cornish cliffs two years ago, whilst on holiday walking the South West Coast Path. Police found no evidence of foul play, but nor any reason for the fall. Fencing protected the cliff edge, Johanna was an experienced walker, and no substances showed up in her system. At the same time, a set of three nineteenth-century Finnish landscape paintings disappeared from her gallery. Natalie's Finnish husband had arranged the purchase of the paintings. Organised crime thrived between Finland and Estonia, and Natalie thought her husband may have annoyed the Estonian mafia in obtaining the paintings. The inquest returned an open verdict. Six months ago, Natalie's husband had vanished—which wasn't unprecedented but never lasted this long. Shortly after, an anonymous "friend" of Johanna started sending her letters claiming proof of murder and warning of danger. She would show Rob the letters.

Natalie shifted to the edge of the sofa, leaned across the desk and placed both hands on Rob's left arm. "You'll help me?" she said.

"Well—"

"I know you will."

"I've got a busy caseload." Her eyes made contact with his, lingered. "I need to finish some things off first." She let go her grip and stood up. "I can start on the tenth of September."

"That's ok, I've waited a long time. You're brave—there will be danger."

"I'm used to that."

Natalie left as suddenly as she'd come, leaving a mist of perfume and a business card.

Rob put his head in his hands.

*****

"Marianne." He faced her, a little too close. "I run this as a program. I know how A fits with B and you don't always. When you work with Julie behind my back, you break my control. We don't even understand what those samples are. At least not from your latest report—which is missing a lot."

"I—"

"Sorry if I'm being hard." Professor Wolf stepped back, brushed his hand across his hair. "You do great work, Marianne, and I chose you for a reason. We're at the business end now and need to keep discipline. I have people expecting results."

"I've been so busy, Professor."

He smiled for the first time, placed his hands in his pockets and leaned against the opposite bench. "What were those samples?"

"I'm expecting a breakthrough. Not as far as I hypothesized in the report, but a magnitude improvement in physical performance."

"Excellent. The details are too sketchy in your report. I don't understand why you changed track as you did…although once you made that leap—"

"Sorry. I have an updated report with full commentary. I didn't want to send it before doing some more checks."

"You realise what you're proposing is unstable?

Reproducing identical batches would be hard to impossible."

"At the moment, yes."

"Do you have the samples? Julie's already used what you gave her on our mice." The professor pushed himself off the bench and faced the window. Marianne turned to mirror him. The building lights illuminated the immediate vicinity, which faded into darkness beyond.

"They're at home. I created them last week, I didn't discover anything useful today."

"Do you have any samples on you?" He pulled her rucksack towards him and undid a strap.

Marianne didn't move.

The professor's phone rang. He looked at the number. "I need to take this."

"I have to go now, Mark. I'm meeting someone." Marianne took the rucksack from him.

The professor rapped a hand on the desk and tightened his lips. "Ok. Make sure you send me the report tomorrow." He answered the phone.

She navigated the empty building—through the office and reception room, along the passageway, down three flights of stairs—and forced herself not to run. Once on Broad Street, she hailed a taxi to the station and made her way home.

*****

Rob gave a final wave at the front gate and Kate smiled. One cat returned.

"A celebratory coffee?" she said.

They ended up sitting outside the tea room at St Cross Hospital, the monastic buildings of the Inner Quadrangle to their right. They faced the water meadows and savoured the four o'clock sun, still hot on this last Sunday of August.

"You're enjoying being a detective, aren't you?"

"Well…you know." He raised his sunglasses, replaced them. "Yes. I've learnt a style of sorts—simple but seems to work. I keep digging for information, either using the Internet or asking questions of anyone in the neighbourhood or with any likely knowledge or connection. That leads to more questions or someone else to talk to and eventually a breakthrough. I also cheat a bit and use my powers, usually when I'm searching for something. For the tree and the bike, I flew a bit—which is risky—and used my speed and eyesight to cover the ground quickly."

"How are the cases?"

He counted them off on his fingers. "First was Mrs Jones' tree. I spotted trees cut down the same way in a garden in Fulflood and realised the fourteen-year-old son was responsible. We sent the police round and scared his parents. Second, Mr Deacon's affair-which-wasn't. He developed a sudden zest for life and tried to hide it from his wife, so she didn't feel left behind. She's taken up judo now! Third, and thanks to you working the streets and talking to everyone, the cat's been found enjoying hospitality halfway across town. And fourth, the bike wasn't stolen at all, but moved by the council."

"So that just leaves the international murder, probably linked to the Estonian mafia."

"Er, yes."

"What were you thinking, Rob?" She took a bite of cake and tilted her head towards him. "Did you find her attractive?"

"My interest was purely professional." She continued to stare at him. "Well…maybe a bit…possibly." He smiled. "I don't think that's the main reason. The murder case is a chance for something new—though not yet. It's a different story. I get the impression we're heading for some kind of finale before that. The quest for the Velvet Vandal is personal and takes priority now, and the tennis final is also looming."

"I sense a change in the air as well, though less clear-cut than your superhero showdown. I'm happy that I've improved the physio practice, with the multi-disciplinary group and website both live and going strong. That's part of our routine now, so I should have more free time and be open to opportunity. Not sure what opportunities," she said, with a smile. "Not sure what to do about Arnold either." Her lips pursed. "His messages are mixed, and...I'm not sure how interested I am. He has good points though, and there aren't many single men in Winchester—"

"Um—"

"And of course, you'll need my help to wrap everything up."

"Well, here's to an exciting end to the summer." Rob raised his coffee.

They clinked and Kate said "Cheers." Leaning back, they watched the sun play over the meadows and an out-of-control Dalmation dashing back and forth.

Chapter 14

Rob booked the final days of August and all of September off work, taking advantage of a holiday backlog that had built up. Every year he took a week's trip with an activity company, but otherwise had no firm plans and left holiday booking to the last minute—resulting in an unused week or so each year. This time he felt more focus.

He started researching the detective business early on the Monday. Private investigators were currently unlicensed but that was about to change. The Private Security Industry Act 2001 provided the framework for licensing of the industry. The wheels ground slowly and only now did this look like being implemented. Soon you would need a Private Investigator license from the Security Industry Authority. This would involve an approved qualification to prove competence, and passing the "fit and proper person" test involving identity checks and determination of good character.

Rob hadn't taken things seriously so far, but he realised a lot of training and experience lay behind becoming a skilled investigator. Elements that caught his attention included: interview skills, taking statements, surveillance and recording, database searches (and access to free and subscription databases), court procedures and legal training. And then there was the whole business side—setting up, marketing, satisfying and retaining clients. Rob found himself fascinated. He signed up for an online course with the Institute of Professional Investigators and began right away.

After a couple of modules, he turned his attention to the Velvet Vandal. Re-reading the culture blog and cross-checking against the crimes gave more of an insight into the modus operandi. The Velvet Vandal would choose one of Rob's cultural events and target an object from the blog, often something mentioned as an aside such as the dog—or fox—sculpture in Dean Garnier Garden or the anteater at the zoo. The major exception to this was the Round Table which he'd described in detail in his entry on the Great Hall. This was also the one theft which seemed impossible.

Rob used his analysis to predict the next targets. The top three on the list were the Westgate Museum at the top of Winchester High Street, the Solent Sky Museum in Southampton and the Winchester City Mill. He decided to concentrate on the Westgate Museum, the most obvious items to steal being the weights and measures which had once been used to define the English Standard.

*****

Drizzle, drenched undergrowth and grey skies dominated his horizon. He pushed between two bushes on the narrow path, spray jumping up at him. After another fifty yards of this, the terrain opened out. An expanse of open ground harboured clusters of derelict buildings which fought battles against encroaching vegetation. Wild grasses and vegetation increased in thickness and height the further he looked, the whole area eventually ringed by trees. He saw a beauty and an eerie sense of history in this wasteland and could imagine a thriving and populated past. His phone rang.

He checked the caller id and answered. "Hello. Velvet Vandal."

The voice at the other end displayed exasperation. "I need

you to do something, and I know you're trying to annoy me. This whole Velvet Vandal thing is a distraction. I told you to blend in, not become the biggest story in Winchester."

"I can't stop myself. When the powers are strong in my body, my mind is obsessed."

"It's a side effect of the drug. Strong drives or resentments are intensified. Why you ended up stealing the local culture, I have no idea."

"There is some logic. No harm is done, though. There is romance in my alter ego, no?"

"No. Once you've finished your mission we'll have a new drug that fixes this issue and will give you consistent powers instead of highs and lows."

"What do you want me to do?"

"Shut down our target as discussed. I also need you to get me the latest test tube samples—this is crucial. They should be labelled with a recent date, but take anything you can find. Leave the laptop—I've got the files I want—but take the notebook; that's where we'll find the real unguarded thoughts."

"Tomorrow daytime?"

"Yes."

The call disconnected.

Snatches of sun were breaking through as the rain died away. He headed diagonally left, over a pitted tarmac road and towards a low rectangular brick building barely visible through its camouflage of green. Rabbits scattered before his approach.

The Velvet Vandal *did* bring romance to the city. He had to be seen enough to generate interest, not enough to lessen the mystery. He had to plan and execute daring crimes and keep the story going over the whole summer. And of course there would be a showdown—outcome unknown and to be determined. He relished the intrigue, although downsides existed. For a start, he had to feed this anteater.

Chest-high bushes and brambles guarded an ivy-covered entrance passage to the building. A few feet in, planks of wood fortified by rocks blocked access. He shifted enough debris to squeeze inside. The interior consisted of several rooms connected by open doorways. Light penetrated through windows built into a parapet structure on the roof. Colourful graffiti filled the walls. An anteater tugged at his rucksack.

"Down Hector."

He pushed him away and opened the rucksack. He pulled out a container full of a food mixture—created based on internet research—and tried to empty it into a dog's bowl in the corner of the room. Hector kept pushing at him and clawing the bowl. Half the food ended up on the floor. Hector had grown to almost five foot over the past few weeks. He acted like a boisterous adolescent and even seemed to like his new keeper. Which was lucky because he was a powerful animal and those claws were vicious.

The Velvet Vandal moved to a second room. Straw bedding for the anteater lined the right side. A rectangular padlocked chest sat in the left corner. He unlocked it. Winchester's stolen culture remained safe inside: the sleeping dog sculpture, the eighteenth-century pewter from St Cross Hospital, tiles from the Sparsholt mosaic and more besides. George Shaw's The Unicorn—too big for the chest—stood in a third room, packed in cardboard and polythene and screened by a hefty table-top to protect it from the anteater.

Hector finished the meal and started to pace through the rooms. He stopped to nudge the Velvet Vandal and scratch at the mosaic. The Velvet Vandal decided to let him roam. He had bought a collar and sometimes freed him for the night, within the limits of a fifty metre rope. Nobody came to this area at night and hardly anyone in the daytime. He attached the collar and rope and they moved outside. Hector snuffled off, presumably in search of ants.

He kept half an eye on Hector and pulled up the Internet on his phone. He navigated to Rob Griffin's Year of Culture website. His powers rose and fell in unpredictable manner, but his body always gave forewarning. A tingling feeling had affected him all morning and an increasing suppleness ran through his muscles. This would be mid-level power, the sensation not severe enough to indicate the highest potency. That had only happened once before and he'd taken advantage to steal the Round Table—which he still couldn't believe he'd pulled off.

The impulse to continue the Velvet Vandal legend grew more intense, but, despite his phone conversation, he could resist if he wanted. However, he enjoyed it—and the work wasn't complete yet. He scanned Rob's blog entries and stopped at week twenty-nine.

Week 29 (13 Jul-19 Jul): Westgate and Museum, Winchester

Once again, I left this week's culture until Sunday afternoon. Let me set the scene. Start ascending the upper section of the High Street and you'll go past clothes stores, estate agents, bridal shops…nothing out the ordinary. A couple of opposing trees add colour. Walcote Place on the right has a neat café and quirky shops. Dame Elisabeth Frink's bronze Horse and Rider sculpture sits on the left. This is getting more interesting, but not earth-shaking—until you look up and see the magnificent Westgate guarding the apex of the High Street. This is a twelfth-century fortified stone gatehouse to Winchester, one of two surviving medieval gates to the city (the other is Kingsgate, housing the tiny and superb St Swithun's church above its arch). Different patterns of stonework reveal modifications from the thirteenth and fourteenth centuries, heightening the impression of age. Standing approximately ten metres by ten metres square and about the same height, there's a large arch passageway, which was used by traffic until 1959, and a smaller foot passage.

The interior chamber has been turned into a museum and is reached through an oak door and up a narrow stone staircase. The museum contains a miscellany of artefacts, which include a painted Tudor ceiling, ancient armour and weapons, and a set of physical weights and measures previously used as the English Standard (known as the Winchester Measure). The latter include quart, pint, half-pint and quarter-pint bronze tankards and half hundred-weight and one stone weights, and date from the 1300s to the 1700s. Most impressive, though, is the room itself—like a mini-medieval hall with thick stone walls, oak flooring, stained windows and gunports for hand cannon—and the Westgate's history. After its initial incarnation as part of the city defences, it served as a debtors' prison from the sixteenth to eighteenth centuries, the clubroom of the adjacent Fighting Cocks pub, an archive centre, and a museum since 1898. A quick aside on the pub: the Fighting Cocks was demolished in 1837 and a new pub, The Plume of Feathers, built on the same spot, only to be pulled down in 1938. My fascination here is that old and bygone pubs evoke a history of their own—not the drama of defending the city gates, but vibrant places creating communal atmosphere and cheer night after night until suddenly they're gone, the carefree spirit dissipating away.

Anyway, back to the Westgate, and I haven't even mentioned the roof. So…continue up the stairs to reach the battlement level, and find a superb cityscape. The view snakes down Winchester High Street—Britain's oldest, apparently—taking in many heritage sights such as the eighteenth-century Town Clock, the Guildhall tower and King Alfred's statue, before culminating in the tree-shrouded St Giles Hill. After an excellent hour of culture, I retired to the St James Tavern for a swift pint.

Yep, that would do. He could take the weights and measures and escape over the rooftops of the adjacent Register Office and Council Chamber. With some effort he rounded up the anteater, and then backtracked to his car and drove into Winchester.

*****

"Another cup of coffee?"
"That'll be my fifth. Do you think that's safe?"
"As long as you have a piece of cake with it."

Rob smiled. "Go on then."

He had an outside seat at the café in Walcote Place and a clear view of the Westgate. The waitress brought his order and he went back to the private investigation course on his laptop. He made sure to scan the area every few minutes, although he didn't expect the Velvet Vandal to strike during a busy afternoon.

By five thirty closing, he realised how dull stakeouts could be without a partner. Mind you, he had completed two course modules and enjoyed the intermittent sun. The logical place to decamp to was slightly uphill to The Westgate pub, fifty yards past the Westgate itself. First he killed an hour wandering the nearby streets and Law Courts area, not letting the gatehouse out of sight for long. He wore trainers, stretchable hiking trousers and a fleece with a hood. The mask was in his pocket.

He entered the pub. The bar was quiet, but a number of people sat at restaurant-type tables in various nooks and corners. He ordered an orange juice and lemonade and sat by a window, allowing him to overlook the Westgate. After another hour he'd read through a third module. A red and orange sunset started to develop. A diet coke this time, and Rob abandoned the course and browsed the Internet. A further hour and a half, and twilight was running out. About twenty people occupied the bar area now, in separate clumps. He ordered a pint of lager. Just the one. He took a first sip and put the glass down. As he raised his head, a movement from the opposite roof crossed his vision. He peered closer. Definitely a shadow and then it was gone. He pushed to the bar and handed his laptop to the barman.

"Can you look after this please?" he said. "I'll be back."

Rob dived across the road to the foot of the Westgate. The

movement had come from the left side, near the top of a more decayed section of wall. He circled the structure and checked the entrance doors. Both were locked and secure. He faced the building from the front, the downhill side. Three men, early twenties, walked up the High Street on the opposite pavement; a couple held hands further back on his side. He pulled up his hood and readied the mask. The men passed him, then the couple. He took a deep breath, put on the mask, and half-flew, half-climbed the face, tumbling over the parapet onto the flat roof.

Wooden decking lined the roof and he rolled across it, coming to a crouching pose in the centre. Lights from the street and surrounding buildings half-illuminated the top. Each corner was about three strides away. A head-high wall faced him; a short section of sloping roof extended above it, terminating at the limit of the Westgate. A triangular annex jutted out on his front left and stretched beyond to encompass a rooftop vista of jagged, oblique and tower-like shapes, leading towards the Great Hall. The side of the annex held an oak door, shoulder-height, which stood open a few inches. Wood around the lock was splintered and a heavy bolt near the bottom hung off at an awkward angle.

He gently drew the door further open, ducked his head and stepped inside. A stone stairway led downwards. A noise disturbed the stillness—a metallic clang, followed by soft footsteps. He descended a few steps and the stairs turned left. The noise stopped. Less light found its way here, but his improved vision picked out the features. Fifteen narrow steps led to a patch of oak flooring. To the left would be the interior chamber and museum. A figure appeared on the lowest step. And stopped.

Rob hadn't seen battle action as a superhero and felt uncertain. He waited for the first move. The figure wore a cape with a hood, a mask and dark clothing, and held a rucksack. It moved up a step. Rob moved down a step. His opponent was about five foot nine and athletic without being over-muscular. He assumed a man. They each advanced another step. His heart rate soared. He tried to think of this as sport, a tennis match—working out how to play the opponent, when to attack and defend. A further step. The clanging sounded again, the cause now clear—objects in the rucksack colliding. One more step. They were in touching range. The figure spoke.

"We're not due to meet yet."

The voice was male and sounded unnatural—flat and low-pitched. Rob got the impression he was hiding an accent.

"You know who I am?" Rob said.

"Culture Man."

"You're the Velvet Vandal."

"The same."

Rob kept his senses on high alert, watching for any change. "What's in the bag? Why are you doing this?"

"Bronze tankards from1719. Winchester's quart, pint, half-pint and quarter-pint measures. You'll know all about them."

"Put them back."

"Why I'm doing this…."

There was a blur of motion. The rucksack had been hurled to Rob's right. Rob slowed it with half a hand. The Vandal accelerated to Rob's left, swerved at the last moment as Rob moved to counter, and dived at the narrow gap on his right. Rob spun and tackled him below the knee. The Vandal struggled free and scrambled upwards, grabbing the rucksack on his way. Rob followed. At the point the stairs turned right towards the exit, the Vandal pushed against the wall and found some extra acceleration. Rob flailed at his heels, missed. The Vandal burst through the door and tried to slam it behind him. Rob took the brunt on his shoulder but held firm and pushed his way onto the rooftop.

They faced each other. Rob backed towards the annex, guarding the way across the rooftops. The Vandal stood in the centre, nowhere to go. Rob detected a hesitation. He started to feel the situation was just as new to both of them. His confidence grew. The Vandal clearly had powers akin to his own, but the skirmish on the stairs suggested an equal, and not superior, speed and strength.

He scanned the surrounding environment. Empty upper-floor offices and council buildings stood to the left, the law courts to the right. The walls to their front and rear shielded them from the streets; only a twenty yard stretch of Tower Street afforded visibility from below and no one was there.

"How did you steal the Round Table?"

"You're impressed?"

"You want me to be? Where is it?"

"It was not easy." The Vandal stayed loose on his feet, continually making micro-movements in all directions but with a subtle bias to the left. He shrugged. "My abilities change, sometimes like a lion, sometimes less. Yours I think, stay the same."

Rob anticipated a vault over the railing to the annex roof, and shifted right to counter. "People care about this culture. What you're doing has no merit."

"People care more when it's gone."

"Not true, not for many. There's no reason for this." Rob inched forward. He shouldn't be too passive and wait to defend, he should try to attack.

"You'll find I'm doing Winchester a service. The reason is for you to discover."

Rob pushed his right foot onto its toes, the calf muscle taut. "What's with the cheap cape," he said.

"It is not cheap!" The flatness left the voice and the edge of an accent crept in. "This is the finest velvet—"

"As for those leggings—"

They moved simultaneously. Rob launched forward, aiming a rugby tackle at his midriff. The Vandal exploded upwards and left, catapulting over the railing. Rob caught him from the side. The momentum flung them both over the railings and to a hard landing on the annex roof. The rucksack clanged like crazy. They rolled upwards before coming to a precarious halt diagonally across the roof's slope. Rob's left hand pushed against the tiling, scrabbling for purchase. His right arm hooked around the Vandal's waist, above him, and he tried to pull him over the top and down the slope. Succeeded. The Vandal smeared his body against the surface to stop himself sliding any more. Keeping a grip on the rucksack inhibited him. Rob reached for the rucksack and they jointly held it. This equalized their balance, and the Vandal brought his other hand into play and pushed Rob back. They wrestled across the rooftop, sometimes rising to a kneel, sometimes rolling, all accompanied by the crashing and chiming of the tankards.

Fighting at close quarters on such a surface made it difficult to use any exceptional speed or power. Shouts dimly penetrated their arena. The Vandal gained a precarious balance and forced himself to his feet. Rob twisted to follow and caught sight of a group of people on Tower Street, pointing up. The Vandal kicked back and he felt a hammer blow in his chest. He struggled for breath. The Vandal thrust forward and accelerated over the annex, across the flat roof above and towards a window box poking out on the left. Rob forced a breath in. He took a couple of thrusting, skidding steps against the roof and launched into flight. Thirty yards low over the roof and he caught The Vandal in a shelter between two opposite-sloping roofs, then grabbed the rucksack with both hands. They pulled and yanked, full power now. The rucksack split and Rob tumbled back, a couple of bronze tankards following him. He hit his head on the corner of the window box and lay disorientated. The Vandal sprinted to the edge of the roof and kept going, his motion turning to flight, and he disappeared over the Great Hall and beyond.

After twenty seconds or so, Rob lifted himself up and checked his body. A cut and a throbbing on the back of his head, but generally ok. The tankards rested on the flat area of the roof. He picked them up and placed them at the top of the stone staircase inside the damaged door: a pint and quarter-pint tankard. The Vandal must have got away with the quart and half-pint.

Police sirens sounded. He retraced his route to the window box and flew down to the courtyard outside the Great Hall. The area was empty and peaceful. He descended Romsey Road to the pub, retrieved his laptop, finished his pint and walked home.

Chapter 15

Seven o'clock Tuesday morning, 31 August. Only partially-refreshed from the shower, Marianne stumbled against the kitchen table as she simultaneously towelled her hair and reached for the overhead cupboard. Creating a sanitized version of the Project Hermes report—still not sent—had kept her up late. She poured the last of the muesli into a bowl. Added milk. Made a cup of tea. The ringtone of her phone sounded. She followed the noise to the bathroom. The display showed Julie, the PhD student from Oxford.

"Marianne, I'm so sorry. I didn't mean to tell the professor about those samples, not until we'd discussed the results. He insisted on knowing everything. I haven't seen him like that: intense, but without the charm. I couldn't hold back."

"Julie, don't worry. I understand. I think he's under a lot of pressure, but he has shown a different side lately."

"I know. He shouted at a tutorial group yesterday. He's normally laid back—in his charismatic and commanding style, of course. All the students fancy him."

"They do?"

"Yes. I mean he is mid-forties but doesn't look it. We don't think he's got a partner at the moment."

Marianne put a piece of bread in the toaster. She moved to the spare room, phone to ear, and hastily crammed work stuff into her shoulder bag. She didn't have time for this, she had a presentation to give today, but….

"I always assumed he had an equal-status partner—a top lawyer or something. I never asked. Any other gossip?"

"I heard a rumour he has a son from a youthful liaison.

Though there's nothing online."

"Really—"

"Yes, but Marianne, I'm sure you're busy and there's something else. Early results from testing your samples on the mice are in."

"Already? I thought the effects would take a few days to show."

"They can fly."

The toast popped up. Marianne didn't say anything for a moment. "Aeroplanes?"

"No."

"What do you mean—?"

"All the neuromuscular tests are amazing. The grip strength test we've been using measures twelve point six. Their speed on the wheel is up to thirty kilometres an hour. Then we tried a jump test, food ratcheted up to different heights, you know the setup. Once I reached half a metre, the action changed. The mice stopped jumping, they took a couple of steps and launched themselves. I increased the horizontal distance, and Marianne, they flew. Their bodies stayed taut and they soared. One of them travelled fifteen metres. The two samples don't show any significant differences."

"Does the professor know?"

"Yes. Strangely, he didn't seem surprised about the flying. He did expect more erratic behaviour, but everything's been consistent and repeatable—for a day at least. He's shut off access to the lab now, I can't get in."

"What! Why?"

"He said he needed to run some experiments himself. I'm not meant to contact you."

"That's insane. There must be a misunderstanding. Julie,

thanks for the call. Work's a nightmare today, but I'll try and speak to the professor later. I won't mention this conversation. Can you let me know any updates?"

Julie promised to keep in touch with further developments.

Marianne ate the toast. A quick brush of her teeth and a hurried exit to the car. She switched the ignition on. The phone rang again. An unknown number this time. She couldn't decide whether to answer, but in the end grabbed it.

"Hello."

"Hello Marianne. This is Jerome."

"Jerome?"

"Yes, we met in Bordeaux. I got your email."

"Ah Jerome. Of course. Great to hear from you." She put the seatbelt on.

"I called you early. I remember your days are busy."

"Yes…you're right, best to get me early." She tapped the steering wheel. "I'm afraid the rest of today is full."

"This sounds familiar, Marianne. We never manage to talk enough. My news career has taken unexpected turns that would interest you."

"I like your journalism. I remember you talking about your specialist interests on the course…."

"How news reporting can shape the story and change events. It is fascinating. I work on your local paper today, and even in this situation—"

"Yes. I'm interested to hear more. I have to go to work now—"

"Then we shall have dinner. Thursday. I will call you."

"Er, yes."

She drove to work, her mind distracted on a number of fronts.

*****

Like waves crashing on a shoreline, advancing until the limits of high tide, polishing and fragmenting along the way, retreating to low tide, and then repeating again…so passes the day. Superficially each day often the same, though sometimes there are storms or amazing calms or a whole medley of contrasting phenomena. But even the days that look the same never are. The waves are different heights, the shoreline subtly changed, the atmosphere altered—time lost in history and never to repeat. Here's the rest of the day, up to about six in the evening.

Rob searched Winchester for inspiration and stolen heritage. Mostly inspiration. Where could you hide a five-metre, one-ton Round Table? He started in the direction he'd seen the Velvet Vandal fly the previous night. Past the hospital and university areas and further afield, racing through the surrounding fields and woods. Maybe an old barn or outbuilding of some sort. He soon slowed to a walk. He could fly over the city and surrounding country at night to get a better—aerial—perspective.

For now, he tramped all over Winchester, trying to think. The Velvet Vandal had said "We're not due to meet yet" and "The reason is for you to discover." There must be a way to make sense of this. He called Kate at lunchtime, gave her a summary of the previous night's adventure. She was pleasingly concerned. At six o'clock he returned to his office and found someone on the sofa waiting for him.

Paul woke to a text from Sarah. It was reasonably intimate, and he smiled. He'd see her for dinner that evening. Meantime, a hectic work schedule faced him. Kelly's adventure company currently ran the software on a month-by-month basis, yet to commit to a permanent deal. Trials with several other companies were running—some paid, some not. He wanted more market penetration before a formal product launch, but you couldn't wait too long or the competition would overtake you. He had a meeting with Ravi about their website revamp and with their marketing consultant on strategy, and lots of leads to chase after last week's newsletter. In parallel, Ravi continued to develop all kinds of software innovations and actually needed to be reined in to keep the product simple. The formal product name for their efficiency software also needed rapid resolution and was proving elusive. The consultant had pointed out various problems with the working title of Robot Helmet.

A quick breakfast and he determined to get as much done as possible today. He should make time for Rob tomorrow. The confrontation with the Velvet Vandal moved events to a more serious plane. Throwing in the approaching tennis final and the prospect of his powers coming to an end made for a challenging period for Rob. Kate hadn't detected any deterioration in the powers so far, and they'd agreed not to say anything until and unless that happened.

He would be disappointed himself if Rob went back to normal. Back in his twenties and early thirties, Paul had been involved in high-adrenaline sports—both surfing and climbing to a reasonable standard. These had tailed off as he got older and focused on other priorities, but he missed them from time to time. Being involved in Rob's adventures brought the thrill back and he relished it. He switched to dynamic professional mode and worked through to six in the evening.

Marianne's day was disappearing in a blur. Emails, meetings, her presentation, ten minutes for lunch and no time at all for the scientific work she really enjoyed. By four, everything that needed to be done had been done. She completed some documentation and debated whether to spend some time in the food processing lab. An incoming email winked on the screen. It was an external email revoking her access to the Oxford biochemistry building. No details and an anonymous do-not-reply sender address. All thoughts of work disappeared. A pattern had been building. Professor Wolf was a powerful man and gradually, over recent weeks, she'd become less comfortable with him. But the latest events were beyond anything reasonable—he now seemed like an enemy.

The thought sank in. Anger rose. She'd worked all hours. Trusted the professor. Her original idea had sparked the project and her insights pushed it forward. Was she being sidelined, her contribution downplayed? Or—the first time this occurred to her—did a completely different agenda exist, one she knew nothing of. After all, their research had the potential for all kinds of use or misuse. Her mind circled, but she could fight this. She still had the samples, her notes and all the knowledge. First thing would be to document everything. She left the office at quarter past four.

Kate had two new patients. One of them played cricket for Hampshire. An hour's session for each of them, plus eight repeat customers at half an hour each. She posted exercises online for the patients to tick off, or printed them out for those without internet access. A new angle on glute retraining worked better than expected and she wrote some notes to add to the website. Seven patients showed solid progress. The exception had an unresponsive RSI-type wrist strain. She added him to the list for the weekly discussions with her group, which was working very well. Case studies amongst a multi-disciplinary team wasn't new, of course—but it didn't happen often enough amongst the jungle of physios, osteopaths, chiropractors, massage therapists, acupuncturists, and more, that many patients found themselves in.

In essence, Kate was at the top of her game—making a difference, innovating, passing on knowledge, enjoying the work. So why did lunchtime find her googling the Estonian mafia, wondering how to help with Rob's next case? Trying to work out where the Round Table might be? Yearning for…what? For excitement? Maybe. Or was she deflecting something: a feeling that still hovered out of reach, that things were more complicated, that they were missing a layer? She shrugged, concentrated on her work and the hours flowed. She wrapped up at six and, thinking about Rob's phone call, dropped him a text, said she'd call round later.

Marianne reached home at quarter to five and apprehension struck immediately she stepped inside. Pure instinct to begin with, but she soon started to notice the underlying rationale. First, the cat was nowhere in evidence. "Spot," she called, softly. Second, the hat stand in the corridor faced the wrong way—her bulkiest coat on the outside, reducing the space to walk past. Either could be explained: Spot could have left via the cat flap, although he didn't often;

the hat stand, well, maybe she misremembered. The kitchen looked normal. She skirted the table and stepped out the other side. The cellar door stood half open. She always locked it.

The key was in the lock and the light on. She pushed the door fully open and slowly descended the stairs, then turned left towards her work area. Only the dim central bulb illuminated the area and shadows scattered across the floor and walls. Silence reigned, and then a mad scrabble and a whir of motion from her front left. A second to realise it was the cat, but a second she didn't want to relive. It took a few moments to control her breathing and allow her heart rate to reduce. She hastened to the spotlights to the right of the worktop and threw bright light over the area.

The logical islands of apparatus on the worktop were wrecked—strewn about and merged together. The packages and bottles on the shelves had been disturbed and some were missing. Her notebook was gone. She checked for something even more important: the crucial samples used in Julie's testing, the culmination of her work. They were kept in the dwarf cabinet against the back wall, beyond the shelves. The lowest draw ought to be locked but had been forced. The samples were gone.

Her laptop still rested on the worktop. She carried it upstairs, picking up Spot on the way, and sat at the kitchen table. A quick check on the laptop showed her files to be intact. With an effort, she could rewrite all the knowledge from the notebook, but…so what? She'd lost her samples and had no way to reproduce them. She no longer worked with an international name able to open doors and give her work credibility. The possibility of using the resultant powers for her own purposes, to do good—even if she barely admitted the aim—was gone.

She couldn't go to the police. Surely Professor Wolf was behind this—although why?—but the tale was fantastical and how would they believe her over a top Oxford professor. She was out of avenues and, as weariness settled over her, reached the edge of tears.

She stared at the calendar a while. A resolve grew and her despair lessened: keep calm and think like a scientist, there's always a solution. She got up, fed the cat, made a cup of tea. Looked at the calendar again…and saw an option. Not a good one, but it was something.

Chapter 16

Six o'clock. Rob crossed his office and turned to stand behind the desk. He placed one hand on the chair back, and used the other to rearrange his notebook and a couple of files. He looked at Marianne, who was leaning back into the sofa with arms folded. She seemed to stare through him and only half-acknowledged him.

"Do you have an appointment?" he said.

She gave the ghost of a smile. "No I don't have a f—"

"Whoa." She still wore work clothes—black skirt and jacket with boots—and her hair was tangled. Her posture didn't alter. "Let me get you a cup of coffee," Rob said. "My sidekick's away, I'll be back in a sec."

"Wine would be better."

He raced up three flights of stairs to his flat, found a bottle of red, and returned to find Marianne standing and studying the Velvet Vandal incident map on the wall. He poured two glasses.

"I want to hire you," she said, without turning round.

"Really?"

"Believe me, I don't have any other options."

"I'll take that as a compliment. What for?"

She turned to face him now, arms still folded. "To break into the private office of an Oxford professor in a secure lab and steal some chemical samples. Take his laptop too, if you get the chance."

Rob put his hands in his pockets. He opened his mouth and paused before he responded. "I'm trying to be a detective. I find things out and help people—following the legal process.

At least that's the idea."

She took a step towards him. "I blurted that out, there's a lot of context to explain. But Rob, you've got superpowers. Your motivation should be to fight injustice, to do good."

"Up to a point." Rob spoke more guardedly now. He recognised a danger he'd end up losing the argument and agreeing to…well, who knew? "I'm not a vigilante, performing criminal acts when I think they're justified. What's the context?"

She switched subject. "Can you fly?"

"Aeroplanes?"

"No."

He smiled. "Yes, I can. Perhaps you can give me the full story."

Marianne had finished the wine. Rob refilled her glass.

"All right," she said. "This is surreal, and I definitely want more information on the flying. It will help us understand what's going on with your body." A pause. "I started working with Professor Wolf eighteen months ago…."

She explained the details of her collaboration with the professor, including the emotional picture. How flattering his patronage was and how she felt a key part of his work. She updated him on the escalation of the project over the summer and how hard she'd worked to drive the next steps, leading to the results from Julie. She tried to describe how the professor had become…more controlling, less a coach. That could be part imagination, but the revocation of lab rights, the current inability to contact him, and the theft from her cellar certainly wasn't.

Rob drained his wine. "You've done all this in your spare time, without telling anyone?"

"Working with a world expert like Professor Wolf is a chance in a lifetime. I didn't question it."

"Are there agreements and emails explaining what's going on? Something to show the police."

"He's been cleverer than I realised. We never had a written agreement. I got a lab pass and a monthly cheque. His emails are careful, they only mention standard research on inflammatory disease—which is all we ever told anyone. Technically, those samples probably weren't even mine."

"Surely the threat of the police would force him to…I don't know, involve you or negotiate."

"He's a more powerful man than you think."

"Yeah," Rob said, a sigh tacked on the end. "Are you sure you've called this right? The Oxford Professor of Biochemistry has used you, cast you aside and sent people to rob your house?"

Marianne hesitated. "Yes."

Silence settled. Marianne half-sat against the back of the sofa. She closed her eyes for a moment and pushed a hand through her hair, tangling it further. Rob paced the garage.

More to delay than anything else, he changed subject. "I ran into the Velvet Vandal last night—which is another story. He's got similar powers to me, including the flying. He said his powers vary in strength, they come and go."

Marianne ran the tip of her tongue round her upper lip, and Rob remembered her cute habit. She looked tired now and spoke slowly and precisely. "My research showed three possible manifestations of these powers. One was oscillatory, like you describe, the changes switching on and off in an unpredictable manner. That was unlikely, and I could never produce the required structure. The other options were long-term—permanent, or several years at least—or short-term and temporary. We can't be certain about your—"

"I think my powers are permanent. It's difficult to explain, but these changes just seem part of me now."

"Maybe. This can't be a coincidence, though. How can the Velvet Vandal be connected to my research?"

"I don't know."

Marianne put her half-drunk glass on the desk. "There must be some intelligence in the professor's office or files to tell us what he's planning and how this all fits together. Once I've got the samples I can analyse them properly. We need to do this tomorrow or the professor will split the samples and complete his testing. Julie should be able to keep us in touch with his movements." She curled her tongue round her lip again. "What are your rates?"

"I'm not a burglar, Marianne, and I doubt I could pull this off. There must be a better way. We can think—"

"We're out of time." She took a deep breath. "You're playing at this, Rob. Low-level stuff. The powers you have are extraordinary. And you're sticking to tennis and finding cats. This is an opportunity to fight for justice. Something truly evil could be happening in Oxford."

He didn't respond.

"Goodbye," she said, and walked to the door.

Rob searched for a balance. The criticism was unfair and he didn't want to back down and appear weak. The plan had disaster written all over it, anyway. And yet. He was aware of not helping, not being bold, missing opportunity. Some decisions gave you time to consider and some needed to be made instantly. Echoes slid through his mind: not returning to the academic career he craved, the opportunity existing anytime in his twenties; not going for that US job, more responsibilities and a good chance of landing it; not asking Laura Perkins out. There were others.

This decision had gone. Marianne had opened the door and stepped through. Head held high. No options left. The door clo—"Marianne."

She glanced round the door and over her shoulder.

"I'll do it."

Chapter 17

Rob spent another half hour with Marianne. She explained the layout of Professor Wolf's lab and office, and, as far as she could, the rhythms of the building—quiet and busy periods, the daily routine. The test lab that Julie had used, prior to being locked out, was in a semi-official, or perhaps completely unofficial, private area in the basement. Normal functioning of the biochemistry lab didn't include animal testing and the professor must have kept it under the radar.

The plan was for Rob to travel to Oxford and assess the situation and the best time to make a move. Marianne would stay behind—to avoid recognition—and provide support and intelligence from Julie on the professor's movements. They debated how much to tell and trust Julie. Marianne would call her and make a judgement.

Three further things happened before the day wound to its close.

First, he called Paul and explained the latest developments. After some initial scepticism and a promise to visit him in prison, Paul generated a spirit of adventure and enthusiasm. In fact, he offered and then insisted on coming with him.

The second concerned Kate. She'd arranged to drop by, but hadn't arrived by eight. Rob walked the twenty minutes to her house, expecting to intercept her at some point. He didn't. Fifty yards away and on the opposite side of the road, he spied her through gaps in the trees. Not a clear view, but enough to see her on the doorstep, hair loose, talking to a man of about the same height. The man leaned forward and kissed her. Damn. Rob kept walking. He soon heard the murmur of conversation. The man touched her arm and then departed. Rob bumped into him outside the gate. "Rob, isn't it?" he said. "I'm Arnold. Kate's told me all about you. I think you're really cool with the tennis and the detective stuff. Brilliant." They shook hands and continued along their respective ways. Rob spent a while talking to Kate. The conversation was pleasant, and he explained their plans for the next day. She wanted to go with them but couldn't take time off work. She didn't mention the kiss.

Third, after he left Kate and as soon as full darkness set in, Rob spent forty-five minutes flying over the city, continuing his search for the missing culture. His heart wasn't in it and he doubted he'd spot the Round Table even if it rested on top of the cathedral tower.

*****

Paul picked him up at seven forty-five the next morning. They both wore jeans and jumpers and looked student-like, as far as possible.

They caught the 8:12 Winchester to Oxford and managed to find a seat, platform-bought coffees in hand. The train left on time and the passengers around them settled.

Rob updated Paul on Marianne's early-morning text. Julie—who she was half-trusting but not telling the full details—had intelligence of a late night visitor to the professor's office and a long discussion. Marianne guessed, or hoped, her stolen items had been delivered. In addition, the professor had been called to urgent meetings today and wasn't likely to show up until mid-afternoon.

"What made you keen to come along?" Rob said.

"How would you cope otherwise? The sidekick's usually the one in control."

"You're still thinking about Hong Kong Phooey and the cat which did the real work, aren't you?"

"Not exactly." Paul sipped at his latte. "Do you want to know the real reason?"

"Sure."

"Helping you out, mate. You shouldn't do something this risky on your own. The extra incentive is that we might not get the chance for this kind of escapade again. Marianne's story is outlandish, but she's given us enough reason to believe this is just."

"Thanks, Paul. I'm with you on Marianne. Her morality is sky-high and she believes what she's telling us. It sounds crazy, but then again, I'm flying about at night and battling a masked villain."

"True." The trolley service passed and they both declined. "Morality or not, there's a danger of getting in serious trouble with the law."

"Yes. My thought is we take this stage by stage. Retrieve the samples and try to discover what we can from the professor's office—if we're challenged we may be able to talk our way out of it. I'd avoid anything like stealing laptops."

"Agreed, and I'm glad you said that." Paul leaned back and looked out the window, a rural landscape racing past. "How did you get on with Marianne yesterday, working through this?"

"Therein lies a story." Rob leant forward, rested his elbows on his thighs. "Last night was a tale of two women. I wanted to impress Marianne, you know be authoritative and cool because…well, you do. Then she challenged me and I acted defensively. I didn't want to go along with her plan, but something happened. Partly she was right, but I also became more aware of her mannerisms and a…vulnerability, which is unusual for her. A sort of familiarity came over me. I mean, I fancy her to a degree, but I felt affection more than romance." He smiled. "Of course, she still got her way."

Paul laughed. "Rob, you're in touch with your feelings. Two women, you said?"

"I went to Kate's house afterwards looking forward to the conversation—the Velvet Vandal encounter, today's mission, throw in a few jokes. Near the house, I saw her talking to someone. Some trees blocked the view, but I saw enough to see a kiss. It was Arnold and I passed him at the gate. I chatted to Kate and put in my jokes and she acted super-friendly, but the point is I was so disappointed—bereft, even. Very different from with Marianne." Rob paused a few seconds. "Trouble is, I'd thought of Arnold as shallow, but he complimented me and came across as a confident, nice guy. Which means I have to back away and leave them to it. Rules of chivalry and love and all that."

Paul seemed to consider several responses. In the end he said, "You're upset aren't you?" and Rob let the question hang.

The train pulled in at 9:15. Rob led them towards Oxford city centre, pausing at a food stall to buy breakfast—two bacon rolls. They ate on the street, strolling towards the central area, defined by a loose triangle of Waterstones, Debenhams and the compact St Mary Magdalene Church and graveyard.

Continuing along Broad Street, bicycles everywhere, Rob pointed out some of the culture around them. The Sheldonian Theatre and Bodleian Library on the right, the sixteenth-century White Horse pub on the left. They turned left onto Parks Road, soon passing Wadham College on the right, one of almost forty quadrangle-dominated, historic University colleges. After the college, trees lined the street, and they were well away from the city bustle. A right turn just shy of the Oxford University Museum of Natural History put them on South Parks Road, where the New Biochemistry Building should be.

Rob pulled out some notes. "Right, the entrance is a couple of hundred yards down the road on the left."

Beyond the impressive Rhodes House on the right, they reached an open gate across a narrow side road. The road led through a campus area with chemistry buildings to each side and hundreds of bikes racked wherever a bike rack would fit. After a hundred yards, another road wound left and their destination stared at them.

The all-black rear of the building faced them, a derelict patch of wasteland in front of it. The road led past the side of the building, and its architectural glory shone. Sunlight glinted off multi-coloured glass fins. Pattern and colour effects constantly shifted as they got closer. Past the front corner, a courtyard or piazza containing wooden tables and benches had been carved out of the otherwise square structure, with the main entrance set within. A circuit of the building revealed its impressive size—probably about sixty metres square, with four floors above ground and two below. Three sides were made of glass, all with the reflecting fins. Older research buildings stood around—some with turrets. They returned to the courtyard and sat at one of the tables.

September sunlight angled between the surrounding buildings and created patterns of sun and shade. The lower sections of the walls in this annex were white glass, before giving way to transparency and colour. Artistic patterns etched on the glass resembled insects, although that may not have been the intention. The entrance doors stood open, but the way the light played meant the inside appeared black.

They soaked up the sun. Paul faced the entrance and Rob sat sideways on the opposite bench. A few student-types—early twenties, jeans, coats of all flavours—entered and left the building, but it was outside undergraduate term time and the area remained quiet.

Rob explained the logistics. "Once you go in, a card-activated turnstile controls entry, but should be off from nine to five. Anyone can sit in the café on the other side. Beyond that you need a badge to access the labs. Marianne had one but it's been disabled. There will be CCTV somewhere, but the theory is the professor has much to hide and won't want to drag security into this."

"I didn't see any other entrances. Is this door"—Paul pointed forwards—"the only way in."

"Apart from three fire escapes, but they're only good for going out. Our best plan is to go in about noon when it's busy for lunch and tailgate a student into the labs. Then search the professor's lab and office on the top floor, and the test lab in the basement, find the samples and whatever information we can, and escape."

"Sounds simple enough."

"It does, doesn't it? I left out the hard parts."

They turned to half-watch two students, one male, one female, who had intercepted each other at a nearby bike rack. A debate about cycle helmets struck up as they locked their bikes. The woman didn't have one. She was about five seven, shoulder-length brown hair and didn't wear a coat, just jeans and black T-shirt. They started towards the doors and the man said, "You wouldn't not wear a seatbelt, would you?"

They didn't hear the woman's response, but, as the couple crossed the courtyard, Rob smiled and said, "Seems pretty safe round here."

The woman smiled back and the man frowned. Five seconds later, they disappeared inside and out of view.

"Aren't we meant to be inconspicuous?" Paul said. "Now, what are the hard parts?"

"Ah yes. The professor's office and lab is in a private wing past a reception room staffed by his admin, Geoff, who Marianne thinks is hostile and mixed up in this. The test lab isn't such a problem but will probably be locked."

"So we wait for Geoff to go to lunch or arrange a distraction, and we might have to force a door. We can always pretend we're lost and the lock was already broken."

"You're relaxed about all this," Rob said.

"I'm trying to convince myself. It's only half ten, plenty of time to get nervous."

"Much appreciate the support, Paul. You've helped me a lot. There must be something I can do for you?"

"Well…a couple of things, outside getting me a super-yacht. I'm still seeking the right name for our software and the product launch is fast approaching. If you can think of anything…."

"Absolutely, I'll do my best. Maybe this laboratory will inspire us."

"The other thing is—if we're battling villains, we should have some type of routine to work together. For example, if you're cornered, a code word meaning you're going to throw the test tube to the left for me to catch, or—"

"What a brilliant idea."

They spent the next hour trialling a series of athletic manoeuvres around the piazza and surrounding area. Signals or codes precipitated rapid moves to the right or left, or dives to the floor, or leaps onto benches. Paul's keys stood in for a secret chemical formula to be thrown between them. Feints and distraction techniques were added, and there was even a forward roll and a "run like hell". They weren't experts, but they added a layer of communication that hadn't been there. When someone passed, they placed hands in pockets and feigned a study of the local architecture. Typical superhero and sidekick playing in the sun, waiting for their mission to start.

They went in at quarter to twelve.

Chapter 18

A porch area lay through the external doors, leading to a reception area. Turnstiles led onwards. A sign said the barriers were open for access to the café area, but the doors to the atrium were on twenty-four hour closure. News and lecture details cycled through a loop on a TV screen on the wall. A seminar on "Re-engineering riboswitches and the interaction between cytochrome c maturation proteins" was scheduled for twelve thirty.

The café was a spacious bright area with white tables and plastic chairs. Students occupied half the tables, laptops and phones much to the fore. They decided to eat and moved to the serving counter. Rob ordered the star course of lentil and vegetable stew, and Paul chose a tuna mayonnaise baguette. They found a table and assessed the route into the lab.

A short corridor stopped in front of a closed door, controlled by a card reader on the wall. Two people went through the door in short succession, each pressing a badge to the reader. Soon after, a pair of chatting female students followed and held the door open for a man a few steps behind.

"Doesn't look too hard to follow a group in," Rob said.

"True," Paul said. "Trouble is, we may only have one shot. If someone does challenge us, we'll attract attention."

"Mind if I join you?"

It was the girl without the helmet. "Sure," Rob said. Paul nodded. She put her tray down. She'd gone for the lentil and vegetable stew.

"Good choice of food," Rob said.

"Yes, the main meal's normally good," she said. "What are

you guys studying?"

"I'm particularly interested in re-engineering riboswitches," Rob said.

"My speciality is cytochrome proteins," Paul said, with a glance towards the TV screen.

"Really. What's your approach on the riboswitches? Use RNA aptamers to manipulate the ligand?"

"That's what I usually do," Rob said.

"Me too," Paul said. He introduced them.

Her name was Jackie. "You're not actually studying biochemistry, are you?" she said. "Or anything close."

"What gave it away?"

She had a wide grin and they were safe.

Jackie was at the end of her third year of PhD studies and estimated it would take another six months to complete. She enjoyed the student life, was in the rowing team—not the international team, but about the fifth team down, they had a laugh—and couldn't wait to get out into the world. Her career plans were uncertain, but the biotech company part-funding her would probably offer a job. She had a bewitching smile.

"So, the truth, what are you doing here?" Jackie said.

They both started speaking. Paul gestured for Rob to go ahead.

"A friend of ours used to study here. She told us about the building and its architectural awards. I love culture and historic buildings, but I've never seen modern science architecture. Since we're in town, we took the opportunity. And it's fantastic—the multi-coloured reflecting glass, the sense of space, the older buildings around. My friend said the inside, with the central atrium, is even better…but we don't have access." He stopped.

They both looked at Jackie.

"Hmmm." She leaned back and her eyes twinkled. "I'll do you a deal. I can get you in, but since you've been teasing me you have to come to the twelve thirty lecture."

Jackie swiped her card on the wall and they followed her in. The café's walls had shielded them from the full effects of the light, but here the building's transparent nature dazzled them. The whole central area was hollow, right up to the glass roof. Spoke-like stairs radiated outwards, leading up and down. Multiple laboratories could be seen through glass walls on the upper levels, the technical equipment obvious but the details indistinct. One floor below them was a break-out atrium with comfortable chairs and coffee tables, and two below, the basement, doors and corridors leading off.

Jackie beckoned. "The lecture's now. Afterwards, I've got half an hour to sort some stuff out, so you can nose around and I'll meet you back here." She led them up one flight of stairs, along one and a half corridors and to a room with the sign Seminar Room One.

"You ready for this?" she said, and opened the door.

Attentive students half-filled the theatre, laptops or notebooks at the ready. A screen at the front showed the lecture title and a picture of a complex molecular structure. They sat near the back. Jackie handed them some paper for note-taking. Professor Nicole Schulze started within the minute. "I think everyone understands riboswitches and their basic mechanisms of gene control…."

They staggered out a long hour later.

"I didn't fully understand the part on disruption of

transcription terminators," Paul said.

Rob looked at his notes, which slowly gave way to animal drawings. "I got a bit lost at that point. It picked up with the stuff on tandem riboswitch architectures."

Jackie ushered them down the corridor, suddenly business-like. She pulled them into an empty lab.

"Sorry about inflicting that on you, but I'm impressed. You kept your promise." She brushed her hands over her face and lowered them in an arc. "I have a confession. I'm Julie, Marianne's colleague."

"You must be kidding—"

"I wasn't sure about this—or you—and I have to be careful of my position, but Professor Wolf is way way out of line. The reception room outside his office will be empty in about five minutes. Geoff will go for a baguette at one thirty, or soon after, and I've arranged…distractions. Should be able to keep him away for half an hour or so. The basement lab is locked but a researcher owes me a favour and…"—she shrugged—"likes me. There's a key in the room next door, in the jacket on the coat stand. It has to go back. Best to go there first."

A shared glance and a nod from Paul. "Let's do it," Rob said. "Still meet in half an hour?"

"Yes. I want to be gone long before the professor gets here. Two o'clock, by the exit." She held the door open. And looked nervous. "Shoo," she said, when they hesitated.

They moved quickly. Down three flights of stairs, past the bustle of people heading for their next assignment and a group discussion on the atrium level. The basement area was quiet. Rob followed directions through a maze of corridors. The rooms hinted at secrets here, the transparent glass from the higher floors replaced by solid doors and frosted glass. A man passed them and avoided eye contact—late twenties, glasses and wearing the first white coat they'd seen—then a left turn and the lab was in front of them. Locked, but Julie's instructions worked perfectly. A room on the right provided a coat stand, jacket and key, and they were in.

Faint light infiltrated through a small window at the far end. The room was twelve foot wide and twice as long. Cupboards and drawers lined the right wall. A miscellany of equipment thronged over a central work area. No mice. Paul found the light switch. They'd missed a door, hiding behind a tall cupboard. It led to a long, narrow room. Mice ate, sniffed and generally darted about in a glass-walled pen that covered most the width of the floor. Two cages stood on a surface to the side. One contained four mice. A loose-leaf folder next to them had been left open.

Their main targets were sealed test tubes, three quarters full of a red sticky substance and labelled N13 and N32. In addition, Marianne's notebook and any paperwork that seemed relevant. A quick cast around revealed nothing, although they photographed the later pages from the folder.

Rob checked his watch. 13:37. "We're going to run out of time," he said.

"Let me search this place," Paul said. "You go to the office and I'll join you."

Rob raced most of the way, slowing for the populated area around level one. A passage on the left edge of the top floor led to a reception room. Empty. An oak-looking door on the right had the sign Professor Mark Wolf. A quick knock and he pushed inside. Again, empty. 13:39.

He took in the room, which looked something like the master quarters on a bygone ship. Even a broad-bladed sword in a display case—what was that doing in the Oxford biochemistry department? His search started with the surface areas. He delved behind some clutter on the bookshelves, rummaged through loose papers on the desk, and ran his eyes over the top of pretty much everything in the room. Nothing obvious. A more formal pile of papers on the desk resembled an in tray and he spent some time on this, before dismissing them as standard university business. He switched on the computer and it prompted for a password. A quick try of "blank" and "1234" failed. He figured a successful guess was unlikely and moved to an antique wall-side cabinet, which turned out to be practically empty. There were three sturdy drawers across the width of the desk still to search. The outer two opened and revealed only a flotsam of stationery and a few other innocuous objects. The central drawer was locked and a sharp pull didn't budge it. 13:48.

A second door led to the private lab, where Marianne had given one specific area to check. Rob walked through the door into a large modern lab, eerily quiet, only two other occupants, who either ignored or didn't notice him. Marianne's experimental setup should be at the end of the second aisle, but the surface was clear, presumably tidied away. He checked the shelves under the length of the aisle and scouted the surrounding area. Plenty of open sample bottles amongst the bewildering apparatus, but nothing like the test tubes he sought. He returned to the office.

His phone beeped with a text from Paul—"On my way." He pulled at the desk drawer again. Still locked. A look around the room. Where would the key be—or should he force it.

141

13:52.

Another text. This time from Marianne, who he assumed must be communicating with Julie: "Professor back. Get out."

Rob braced one hand against the desk top and yanked the drawer. The wood around the lock splintered. Another pull and it came free, jamming at two-thirds open. Paperwork sat on top, starting with some invoices. He rooted through the contents: the papers, some bound sets of lecture notes, a science fiction book at the rear, and underneath…gold dust. Two sealed test tubes. The labels were correct. He pushed the drawer inward, then stopped. The invoices had shaken out of alignment and the third one stuck out and exposed a caped man motif near the bottom. The words Velvet Vandal were printed below. With no warning, the door flung open.

Tall and dark, jeans and smart jacket, Professor Wolf stood in front the door and folded his arms.

Rob pushed away from the desk, calmed his breathing. "Is this the physics department?"

Professor Wolf gave a tight smile. "You'll wish it was." He nodded towards the test tubes Rob held. "I don't need those, but you're still going to put them back."

"You're outside the law," Rob said, "and all kinds of ethics." A check of the watch. 13:55.

A second man pushed into the room and stood to the right of the professor. Tall, late twenties and wearing a suit, no tie. Geoff?

The professor's air remained amused. "I doubt the police will think so. You've broken into my office. Vandalised my property. You shouldn't even be in the building."

"Call them, we can chat about your friend the Velvet Vandal."

A brief emotion, a twitch of the mouth. "Any documents you've misinterpreted will be…tidied up. You don't know what you're dealing with." He turned to the second man. "Geoff, call the police—in a minute. Meanwhile, I have the right to defend myself." In one free-flowing move, he flipped open the display case with his left hand, pulled out the sword with his right, and a snap of the shoulder swept it across his body to an aloft position.

Rob flinched, even from ten feet away. The professor advanced a couple of steps. Then another couple. Each time there was a flamboyant series of strokes, vibrations swishing through the air. Rob got the feeling he was playing, but kept razor-sharp attention. The physics of the situation—sword point moving a long way for a short arm motion—meant the blade moved much faster than he could, and he didn't fancy his chances of dodging past. He backed further behind the desk. A thrust this time, across the desk and stopping a foot in front of his chest.

Paul skidded into the room and absorbed the scene: Geoff on his right, the sword situation ahead of him. Geoff attacked and grabbed his collar. Paul chopped downwards and broke the grip. They grappled, holding each other at arm's length, trying to rotate or push backwards.

Rob spoke. "What's your motive? Medical breakthrough and world fame? Nobel Prize?"

The professor laughed. "My plans are more ambitious than you can imagine." Using the adjacent armchair as a launch pad, he vaulted onto the desk and executed a dramatic flourish of the sword.

Paul was finding Geoff stronger than him and tensed his body further to avoid giving ground. He summoned enough energy to join the conversation. "The USB stick I found downstairs tells us more about those plans."

The professor half-pivoted towards him. "I don't think so," he said, but the smile had faded.

Paul caught Rob's eye, who switched the attention back to himself. "We've got plenty of questions to raise," he said. "People will be interested."

The professor turned to Rob again. "We're going to need a serious conversation." An athletic shuffle brought him to the edge of the desk and a lightning sword strike brushed Rob's shirt. His legs tensed to leap down and Rob wasn't sure he was playing now.

Geoff appeared single-minded in seeing his tussle with Paul as a trial of strength—so Paul changed the rules. He loosened his body and let himself be pulled forward, faster than his opponent expected. Lurching sideways, he kicked hard against Geoff's knee, and pushed away, forcing free. Geoff, off-balance, dropped his other knee to the floor. Paul sensed he had a few seconds of respite and gave the signal for left throw.

As the professor leapt, Rob accelerated to his left, beyond the desk, and threw the first test tube. An accurate throw and Paul caught it two-handed. The professor cut off Rob's escape route and Rob darted back to the right, behind the desk—but kept his arm stretched out to leave his hand unmoving as long as possible, finally flicking the second test tube across the room before his arm followed the rest of his body.

The trajectory formed a high spinning loop. Paul recovered balance and reached across his body, intently watching the flight. Geoff grasped towards his ankle. Rob's scramble at the far side of the desk and the professor's pursuit, sword menacing, turned to slow motion as they watched the two-second scene play out. Paul snapped his foot clear, rebalanced with a hop, kept concentrating, and his fingers…knocked the test tube away. His body continued rotating and, becoming airborne to generate the reach, a desperate second attempt pulled it round and against his chest. He saw Rob signal "run like hell" almost before he landed. An instant push-off with his toes, a deceptive body swerve, and he avoided Geoff and sprinted out of the room.

Geoff followed. The professor and Rob faced each other.

The professor stepped back and laughed, sword half-lowered. "Your friend won't escape the building—not that it's important. Nothing you can do will damage me. But I'd rather the formula stayed here. Your female friend is…reckless. Do you know what she plans?"

Rob opened his mouth to speak, but a glimpse at his watch changed his mind. 13:59. He accelerated with full power, a brief hand on the desk and a diagonal leap over and away from the professor, then phenomenal speed to the door, veering to avoid a final swipe of the sword.

He raced through the reception room and passageway, opened the end door, and descended the topmost stairs five at a time. His eyes swept over the scene on the levels below: Julie leaning against the ground floor wall, six yards short of the exit; Paul hurdling down the final set of stairs; Geoff bouncing against the railing, half a second behind.

Julie walked towards the exit door. The wall reader was six feet short of the door. She timed it brilliantly, didn't look back and didn't acknowledge them. She pressed her badge to the reader. Rob streaked past them all and pulled the door open. Paul tumbled out after him. The quickest of backward glances and Rob saw Julie follow, but not Geoff, then they were both through the café and reception and back in the courtyard.

And that was it. They ran until they'd left the campus behind, but no one pursued them. They reflected on events over a pint in the narrow, low-beamed White Horse. A text from Marianne arrived to say "Well done guys and sorry about the deception—Julie safe at home." Their train pulled back into Winchester at 17:24.

Chapter 19

They all met early the next evening to discuss plans and strategy. The samples were in a secure location at Marianne's work laboratory. Rob had spent a fruitless day searching for signs of the Velvet Vandal, and everyone else had been working. The venue was Rob's office (or garage). He'd provided a packet of Pringles and an extra chair. The kettle boiled and he poured coffee to order.

"Julie did a terrific job," Paul said, "despite an initial lack of trust."

"She sends her love," Marianne said.

"Fantastic," Rob said, and Paul gave a thumbs-up and a wink.

"She's got a boyfriend—about fifteen years younger than you two."

Rob sighed and exchanged a glance with Kate, who laughed. Then he said, "Not the guy arguing about the helmet?"

Marianne nodded. "We thought that would attract your attention. He did a lot of work holding Geoff up."

Kate sat in Rob's master chair behind the desk. Marianne was sprawled on the sofa, legs over one of the arms. They'd met for the first time and had already engaged in a five-minute conversation on anatomy. Paul sat on the spare chair, trying to extract a single Pringle. Rob stood centre-stage.

"I think Rob, as the detective, should lead the discussion," Paul said.

Rob moved to the whiteboard, marker pen in hand. He'd written a number of headings and he pointed at them as he spoke.

"First thing is the police. I think we've concluded not to involve them for now. We'd struggle to be believed and, if my powers become known, I'd end up under massive scrutiny. Everyone agree?"

They did.

He summarised the rest of the board. "There are several key questions. What's the professor planning? What's his link to the Velvet Vandal? What should we be doing, and are we under threat or do we need to take precautions? Paul, what are your impressions?"

"Since Professor Wolf attacked you with a sword, you'd have to think he's borderline insane. But he seemed confident and in control, as if he knew he could get away with it." Paul took another couple of Pringles and placed the tube on the desk in front of Kate. "He said he had plans 'more ambitious than we can imagine'—but no idea what."

"He sounds like a high-functioning psychopath," Kate said. "I've studied psychology to help understand patients. There's a famous study that says one in five CEOs are psychopaths. They're charming and intelligent, but manipulative and lacking empathy. They evaluate people and situations for their own advantage—sometimes acting out long-term plans which no one else has any idea about. There's also a tendency for high-risk behaviour because they don't expect to be caught."

"With the benefit of hindsight—that could all be true," Marianne said.

"Any thoughts on what those plans are?" Rob said.

"I assumed he was going to present our research on disease mechanisms, and hint at wilder effects. He spoke about working towards a September conference, but I haven't seen any evidence of one. I'm talking to Julie and one or two others to try and understand his diary and his contacts. But we might be way off—maybe he's going to generate world headlines by unveiling superpowers or…sell them to a military power."

"Do you think he's managed to create workable drugs?" Rob said.

"Thanks," Marianne said, pausing as Kate handed her the Pringles. "Impossible to tell, as he clearly kept a lot from me. The source of the Velvet Vandal's powers must come from the professor, so that proves he has something…but those powers are flawed and unpredictable. I'm not convinced he's got anything more, partly because he pushed me so hard for my research and partly I'm starting to think the samples I produced are a giant fluke. I'm not sure they're reproducible."

"One question: what are you intending to do with those samples, Marianne?"

She hesitated. "They need further study. There are some tests and investigations I can run at work."

"Ok. Any luck with the USB stick from the lab, Paul?"

"It's protected. I asked Ravi to try and access the contents and I expect he will."

"Excellent," Rob said. "The other angle is the Velvet Vandal. If I can find him or his hideout that should give us a line back to the professor."

"I'll help you with that," Kate said.

"Thanks." Rob watched the Pringles pass from Marianne to Kate and then on to Paul. "Pass them here," he said.

Paul threw him the tube.

"I may be able to get some information too," Marianne said. "Jerome's invited me to a meal tonight—"

"Jerome?"

"The journalist, the guy who writes all the Velvet Vandal stories. He must have some theories."

"Is that a date?" Kate said.

"He probably thinks it is." Marianne gave a half-laugh and shared a knowing smile with Kate.

"His latest, in today's paper, is interesting," Rob said, moving on. "A witness saw some of the battle on top of the Westgate and took a picture. Culture Man is mentioned. Jerome must have cross-checked the picture from the cat rescue. He writes as if Culture Man and the Velvet Vandal are destined to clash again, with his usual idiosyncratic style—'be assured I will be present to faithfully report developments'."

They discussed security next and concluded Marianne was at risk due to her links with the professor and since she'd already been burgled. Kate offered to put her up and Marianne accepted.

Rob summed up, ending with "Shall we say same time, same place tomorrow?"

They agreed, and Paul reminded Rob he'd need to fit in some tennis training with the final coming up on Sunday.

Kate said "Good luck", and Marianne said, with surprising vehemence, "Make sure you demolish Roger."

"Er, thanks," Rob said, "and good effort everyone." He took another Pringle. "One question on Professor Wolf before we go."

"Yes?" Paul said, and the others looked at him.

"Is he working with others—or is he a lone wolf?"

Chapter 20

The rest of Thursday evening turned rainy. Rob watched TV and planned for an early night, mindful of Paul's instructions to sleep well leading up to the final. Kate set up Marianne in the spare room and gave her a key. Otherwise her plans were pretty much the same as Rob's, with a bit of paperwork thrown in. Paul called in to see Sarah. He was looking after Liam tomorrow, to cover for a combination of her business meeting and the usual childcarer being away. She went through arrangements and fixed him a snack. After a hectic day at work and yesterday's Oxford exploits, he also fancied a relaxing evening and left early. The forecast for Friday and through the weekend was good, auguring well for the Hampshire Cup final, and, for a while, promising to defy the shortening days and the running down of summer. Events surrounding superpowers, the Velvet Vandal, local culture and Professor Wolf continued their course—starting with Marianne's date with Jerome that evening.

*****

"You still search for a way to make the world better, Marianne. And you're scared you won't find it."

"I told you that? And you remembered?"

"I read between the lines. You were tired."

Jerome had booked Loch Fyne in Jewry Street. They sat at an upstairs table overlooking the lower floor. Sixteenth-century beams criss-crossed the restaurant. Rain fell steadily outside, the sound audible but mostly disappearing into the background. They'd almost finished their main courses.

"Your theory about how journalism shapes events…" Marianne said. "You've written a lot about the Velvet Vandal. Do you think he's changed his plans based on the coverage?— playing to the gallery, perhaps? Any idea who he—or she— is?"

"Good questions. But first you must tell me more of yourself. Why are you scared?"

"I'm not." She wore jeans and black blouse, gold hoop earrings. Jerome kept looking into her eyes.

"But something, Marianne." He poured the remaining wine from the bottle and looked expectantly at her.

"Frustrated. I work hard and do my best, but what if I'm doing the wrong things? I'm trying to understand disease in my work—my independent work—but maybe I won't solve the big problems and help people. Maybe I should do something else. Work as a nurse, or volunteer in the developing world, or make a difference in politics—"

Jerome touched her arm. "You will have a beautiful story Marianne. It is certain. And you have beautiful eyes."

Marianne smiled, laughed a little. "That ought to sound corny. But it was nice, thank you."

"I am always sincere." Jerome let the silence settle, then said, "Let me ask you a question?"

Marianne nodded.

"What would you do if you had superpowers?"

"What wouldn't I do?" she said.

Jerome leaned towards her. "I shall tell you about the Velvet Vandal," he said.

*****

Kate met him in Greens Wine Bar for a coffee, early the next afternoon. Jeans and a sweater, hair tied up. The bar functioned more as a café during the day, and they had an inside window seat. She bounced on her toes before she sat down. "Got the rest of Friday off," she said. "I had some ideas about your next case. And thought we could go through the Velvet Vandal files."

"Wow," Rob said. "I'll promote you to chief sidekick."

"Overall commander, I was thinking. Any progress today?"

"Not yet. I'm waiting for Paul's update on the USB stick and any information from Marianne on Professor Wolf's plans. I've been going through this"—he pointed at a map spread over the table—"trying to work out where the stolen items might be stashed, especially the Round Table."

"Any clues in what the Velvet Vandal said to you?"

"Not sure. He said we were due to meet, so he must be planning a confrontation. I want to find him first."

"Perhaps there's an obvious place for the meeting. Does anywhere in your blog stand out, that he hasn't visited yet?"

Rob paused a moment, then rapped the table. "Yes, it does," he said. "The Cathedral. The most obvious symbol in Winchester. Brilliant, Kate. I did a tour of the Cathedral tower and roof for one of my cultural events."

"Maybe a showdown at the Cathedral, then? We…you need to be careful, Rob."

"True. I can't just wait for him, though—I need to locate his hideout. But we can recce the Cathedral to be ready for…whatever."

Kate finished her coffee, stood up and pulled at his arm. "Come on then," she said.

*****

Paul paced up and down, talking on the phone. Ravi hunched over a laptop at the dining room table. Liam played on the iPad—in theory an educational game where a squirrel taught maths, but suspicious explosion-like sounds kept repeating.

Paul put the phone down. "Yes," he said, pumped his fist in the air and slapped the table in front of Ravi. "Want the news?"

"Hang on a minute," Ravi said. "I've almost got this USB." He was younger, twenty-nine, with a recent and well-trimmed beard.

Paul turned to the other end of the table. "How about you, Liam? Do you want an update on our business?"

A prolonged cheering broke out from the iPad, complete with horns and fireworks. "Yeah," Liam said, without looking up. "I'm on level four."

"You're meant to be doing maths exercises."

No response for a while as his hands rapidly jabbed at the screen. "I am. This is shapes."

"Really—"

"Got it," Ravi said. "I could access most the files a while ago, but I found a hidden folder I couldn't get to."

"Ravi! We've won an order—eleven thousand pounds, including one year's support and a weeks' consultancy."

"Brilliant, man. That's the tax firm?"

Paul nodded and they high-fived. "Put it there, Liam," he said, and raised his hand to Liam, who diverted his attention long enough for a cymbal-like clash of hands.

"Expecting Vialta Engineering within the week," Paul said. "That means two different industries we have exposure in. Still waiting on Kelly though." He peered at the laptop. "What are the USB files?"

Ravi shifted to give him a better view. "The files in the main directories are either teaching notes or published scientific papers. I don't understand them but they seem normal, not suspicious."

"And the hidden folder?"

"There are six files. Only one is cleartext, called "Hermes", and gives a list of five entries. The other files must relate to the list since the filenames match the entries, but I can't read them—they're hex, compiled code of some sort."

"What does the Hermes file say?"

"Fairly random." Ravi opened the file. It read "tower; national; palace; castle; history."

Paul shook his head. "I'll chat this over with Rob. Meantime we should celebrate our order. How about a game of football in the park and a doughnut on the way back?"

"Yes please," Liam said, bringing his attention back to reality.

"Once you've passed the maths tests, like your mum said."

"They're easy."

Paul ran through the exercises at the end of Squirrel Teaches Maths, lesson 4, and Liam had no problems. "Hmmm, perhaps you can replace Ravi."

"Hey."

"Let's hit the park. You coming, Ravi?"

"I need to finish"—Paul closed the laptop—"sure."

*****

They sat on a stone bench behind the First World War memorial and stared at the impressive west façade of the Cathedral. The nave roof ran the length of the building beyond its triangular profile and, from this angle, hid the tower at the rear.

Kate played with the Internet on her phone. "I wonder where the best place to find information on the Cathedral is," she said.

"That would be my culture blog," Rob said.

"Not the Cathedral website or Wikipedia?"

"They're ok, but they don't have my style. Try about week fifteen or sixteen."

Week 17 (20 Apr-26 Apr): Winchester Cathedral—Tower

Winchester has evolved from an Iron Age settlement, with ancient hill forts in the vicinity, to the Roman town of Venta Belgarum to the medieval capital of England (from about 850 to 1100) to today's "best place to live in the UK", according to the *Sunday Times*. The modern city is packed with history including ancient castles, churches and colleges, the magnificent Great Hall and much else you'll eventually find in this blog. I haven't even mentioned Hockley Viaduct. Despite this, it's Winchester Cathedral that dominates the postcards and I've taken until week seventeen to get here. This week's culture centres on a tour of the roof and tower. You need to take a one and a half hour tour to climb the tower and I joined one on the Saturday. Before we get there, let's step back and talk about the Cathedral in general. My quick caveat is that this is not the definitive guide—there are whole books on just the stained glass! But, almost as good, here's Winchester Cathedral in a sentence: building on today's cathedral started in 1079, although a church was on the site from the seventh century; the nave is the longest in Europe and was remodelled around 1400; Jane Austen is buried in the north aisle; the superbly illuminated, eight hundred-year-old Winchester Bible is in the equally superb and atmospheric seventeenth-century Morley Library; the diver William Walker spent 1906-1911 saving the Cathedral from collapse by working in six metres of groundwater to shore up the walls with bricks and concrete before the water could be pumped out (a terrific story); and, finally, services to the public are held every day, including Evensong, the source of magnificent choral music that echoes through the ancient stone confines.

Back to the tour. Ascending the tower is a two-stage process. First we climbed a spiral staircase near the entrance to reach the interior roof above the nave. This is effectively a glorified loft, but a fascinating and spooky place nonetheless. Ancient beams cross the central space and line the walls. A central wooden walkway extends the entire length of the nave, with a series of twelve-foot-deep, stone-walled, dungeon-like pits to each side—the pattern of the pits mirror the peaks and troughs in the vaulted ceiling below. At the far side is a room that looks like a larger version of the scout hall I used to go to as a kid. This is the carpeted ringing chamber where the bell ringers practice, complete with old furniture, hanging bell ropes, and, for some historic reason, two broad swords, out of reach on the wall. Plaques on the walls commemorate peals, which are sequences of bell rings taking hours to complete. Each bell sounds different and the point is to ring logical sequences without repetition. For example, one method rings the bells in all the different orders possible: for eight bells, the most ever achieved, this is 40,320 combinations and takes eighteen hours, and a single mistake would invalidate the peal—awesome, if somewhat obsessive. Beyond the ringing chamber is the bell room, which houses fourteen bells. The heaviest is almost two tons and the oldest dates from the 1600s (recast from the original bronze in 1937). The clock mechanism is also here, which, although frequently out by minutes, is always reset for New Year's Eve. The second part of the ascent uses an exceedingly narrow spiral staircase that leads to the pièce de résistance—the top of the tower and magnificent views of Winchester and surroundings. I retired for a swift post-culture pint at the nearby William Walker, because it's expected.

"Fair enough," Kate said. "The Cathedral in a sentence— what more would anyone want? Shall we go in?"

*****

Kate spent a couple of hours exploring the Cathedral and surrounding Close with Rob, trying to imagine possible scenarios involving the Velvet Vandal. Rob explained the culture as they went, although she wasn't convinced the

Cathedral Close residents were locked in at night. She left to do some business in town.

Arnold called. They were taking a trip on his boat tomorrow, which was moored at Shamrock Quay in Southampton. He went through arrangements and told her he might be a bit tired—tonight would be a late night, a big deal the department was involved in. She needed to decide soon. He could still annoy her. Trouble was, his plus points were good. He'd invited her to Chicago, coinciding with his next work visit. Hmmm.

About five o'clock, she dropped home to sort a few things before the meeting at Rob's. She'd forgotten Marianne was staying and found her on the sofa, laptop on lap.

"Settled in all right?" she said.

Marianne took a moment, tapping away. "Yes. I bought a few things, put them in the fridge."

Kate noticed some juggling balls on the coffee table. And a packet of Twixes on the sideboard. She moved to the kitchen area and offered a cup of tea.

Another pause. "Yes, please. Thanks again Kate, this is all very kind." Marianne placed the laptop on the coffee table. "I made progress today on the samples, and on understanding how Rob's ended up as he has. There are still mysteries though. Can we go through your performance data again?"

"Yes, I've got the files upstairs, on a USB stick." Kate brought two cups of tea, put them on the table. "I also read the paper you gave me on macrophage activation. I made a few notes." She paused and pushed a hand through her hair. She said, almost shyly, "Do you mind going over a few questions?"

They discussed the paper first, then sat on the sofa, hunched over the laptop, discussing Rob's data. A full hour passed and they realised the meeting was fast approaching.

Marianne summed up her conclusions. "What we're missing is early data, showing the onset of Rob's changes. But the pattern is clear—a rapid initial change followed by stable performance. The flying is difficult to understand"—she shrugged—"but I don't think it's really flying. Rob couldn't stay still in the air. The mechanism seems like rapid muscular thrusts which eventually exhaust him. Plus some learning of how to be efficient and best use the air."

"I think I agree about the flying," Kate said. "Though I'd like to use software to better analyse the motion."

"Good idea. One thing I am sure of—his powers will run out."

"Really," Kate said, after a pause. "There's no sign of any drop-off yet. You expect that to be quick?"

"Yes. Probably a mirror-image of their appearance. They could disappear within the space of a day."

"I hope it doesn't affect him too much." Kate stood and picked up the empty cups. "Trading down can be tough—like going bankrupt or losing a job. I didn't know him before, but I get the feeling he's changed mentally as well. He takes some things in his stride, like flying or…fighting villains, which I doubt is his natural character. Do you notice any changes?"

"He's more confident," Marianne said, "but only so far. He has a tendency to let things happen rather than control events, but I think that is changing. I accused him of not using the powers for anything meaningful. But if you think the other way round, what he's done—like going up to Oxford and battling the professor—not everyone would do that."

Kate pursed her lips. "I think he's made a great effort. He didn't ask for superpowers, and suddenly he has to deal with them—not many people would end up fighting a supervillain high on the city gatehouse. Or trying to win the Hampshire Cup—"

Marianne rolled her eyes, and they both laughed.

Kate said, "Maybe he *could* end up a private investigator, even without the powers. I think he'd like that, but it would be a bold step and the confidence would have to hold."

Marianne looked at her. "Yes," she said.

*****

Paul sat on the master chair, feet on the desk.

Rob held a sword-length stick in his hand. He executed a series of moves, giving a running commentary. "Lunge, parry, withdraw, parry, riposte, dart." He made some of the terms up.

Kate and Marianne came through the door and Paul said, "What time do you call this, ladies?"

"Important business to attend," Kate said. "What's Rob doing?"

"Good question."

"I've been studying fencing on the Internet," Rob said. He leapt and half-twisted to face them, and followed up with the Zorro-like flourish of a "Z" drawn in the air. "After the professor incident, I want to make sure I'm ready for any sword fight."

Marianne shared a glance with Kate and sighed. "Do you think it's likely you'll encounter Professor Wolf, they'll be two swords available and a few hours on the web will make you competitive against a skilled fencer?"

"You never know."

Kate and Marianne sat on the sofa and Rob stood just to

the side, so they were all congregated around the desk. "Luckily there are some Pringles left," Paul said.

Rob started proceedings. "We've four areas to discuss: the hunt for the Velvet Vandal's hideout from me and Kate; updates from Marianne on the professor and Jerome; and details on the USB stick from Paul."

They spoke about the Velvet Vandal first and the theory that he was planning a finale at the Cathedral. Kate and Rob had drawn up a structured search pattern for Winchester, which Rob intended to focus on tomorrow. Paul reminded him they had a morning coaching session ahead of Sunday's tennis final.

"How did you get on, Marianne?" Rob said.

"Interesting news on the professor. I can't find any evidence of the conference that was so important, but he's cleared out his schedule for the rest of September—which is unusual for an academic of his standing and commitments."

"So, whatever he's planning…likelihood is, it's soon?"

She nodded.

"How about your date with Jerome?"

"Which wasn't a date—"

"Protesting too much, Marianne?" Paul said, leaning back in his chair.

She dismissed him with a flick of the hand. "He's intense and cares about journalism. I'm not sure he can help find the Velvet Vandal."

Rob said, "He must have some theory as to who he is, or at least the type of person and the motivation"—Rob paused, but Marianne was silent—"if he's that good a journalist?"

Marianne shifted in her seat. "He's connected with the police and they haven't got anywhere, other than a very fit five-foot-nine male. The Round Table is their top concern and there's no trace. Jerome thinks it's a challenge and a game for the Velvet Vandal, and the motive isn't malicious."

"Half of Winchester's culture's gone."

She shrugged. "Perhaps…he's going to return it. Jerome said he thought something big would happen tomorrow night, but he wouldn't tell me why."

Paul looked at Marianne and leaned forward to say something, but stopped.

"So we should stake out the Cathedral tomorrow?" Kate said.

The Cathedral area would be well-populated Saturday daytime and they decided to set up a rota from four in the afternoon. Two people would be on watch once darkness fell.

Paul updated them on the USB stick, reading out the file list—"Tower, national, palace, castle and history."

"We're not sure this is relevant to anything," Rob said, "but the professor did seem rattled we had the stick. Any thoughts?"

Silence reigned. Rob paced the office. Paul ate a Pringle. Marianne shook her head.

Kate leaned forward, put her arms on the desk. "There is one thing," she said. "When I researched supervillains"—she smiled as they looked at her—"their plans fit into four categories: treasure, destruction, enemies or power play. The first two are obvious. Enemies means defeating a nemesis, usually a superhero, and power play is the basic world domination thing."

After a pause, Rob said, "Which one do you think it is, Kate? Or Marianne, you know him best?"

"Not destruction," Marianne said. "His whole career has been dedicated to driving research forwards and creating solutions. Not enemies, I can't think anyone's opposed him much. Power play is possible—the professor likes to be in charge, but I can't imagine how or what….. Treasure, no idea."

"Looking at the actual words, treasure makes most sense," Paul said. "For example, Tower could be Tower of London, home of the crown jewels. Several choices for National, maybe the National Gallery and a famous painting? Castle and palace could be any of a number of high-profile targets. History…er, Natural History Museum and a dinosaur?"

"To confirm then," Rob said, "the hypothesis is the professor takes September off and goes on a crime spree round the country?"

"Yes," Paul said.

"A dinosaur?" Kate said

"Er, shall we move on," Paul said.

"To be honest, we don't have any other theories," Rob said. "How about we stir things up, send the professor an email. Ask him about…the crown jewels, see if he bites. I can send it tonight if you"—he looked at Marianne—"give me the address." She nodded.

They finalized plans for Saturday before wrapping up. Rob would continue his search for the Velvet Vandal's hideout, with a break for Paul's tennis session. Marianne said she needed the day to further study the samples but would help out with the Cathedral rota later. Paul and Kate had commitments much of the day, but would also be fine for the rota.

Rob grabbed a couple of conversations as they dispersed. First with Paul, who suggested they try to speak to Jerome themselves tomorrow. "I'm not convinced Marianne told us everything," he said, reinforcing Rob's own view.

Second was with Kate, who nudged him to the side of the driveway. "I can postpone tomorrow's trip with Arnold," she said. "We're reaching the end-game here."

Rob made brief eye contact and smiled. "No," he said. "That wouldn't be fair. Go on, have fun—see you at five for your shift at the Cathedral. Bring him if you like." Gave her a quick hug.

Chapter 21

Saturday 4 September. Rob leapt up at 7.30 a.m. He couldn't know for sure but events have a pattern and somehow his subconscious picked them apart and told him today would see the culmination of his battle with the Velvet Vandal. The final of the Hampshire Cup followed tomorrow, giving him a chance to win a first-ever sports tournament. Completing a hat-trick of challenges, next week saw the start of the Natalie case—which he had no idea how to approach. The uncertain outcome of all three left him feeling alive, the future to be written and not trudged through. Kate being out with Arnold cast the only shadow, but…that was only fair and a superhero shouldn't have much trouble finding a girlfriend. In fact he retained a slight suspicion Arnold was the Velvet Vandal, irrational though that may be. This replaced his theory it was Roger—probably too tall, but how else did he win the Hampshire Cup each year?

Rob's thoughts leapt further ahead. He'd hardly touched his powers yet. He hadn't saved lives or explored…unexplored wildernesses. Perhaps he could run the detective agency as dual purpose: partly a local business, and partly a vehicle to pursue projects and escapades overseas. Whatever, he needed to define plans and explode into action. Just getting by had reigned for too long. One thing at a time, though. He tapped the window sill, spun towards the door and departed, supervillain search plan in hand.

*****

"Trigger," Paul shouted. Rob stepped in and powered a shot to the backhand corner. Paul blocked the ball back, but Rob advanced to the net and put it away cross-court. The time approached noon and they neared the end of their final tennis preparations. Warmth shone down as a half-clouded sky shifted to expose the sun.

The morning search hadn't uncovered any evidence of the Velvet Vandal, but Rob wasn't concerned. The search pattern made sense, and if visible signs existed near Winchester he should find them. Kings Worthy was the afternoon target. However, a hunch told him the most promising area would be around the empty spaces and farmland of Oliver's Battery and Compton, to the south west—the direction the Vandal went after their Westgate encounter. He'd saved that for the evening, when he could risk flying.

They stepped off court and stood to the side of the clubhouse at River Park. A springer spaniel dodged past them. "Good session," Paul said. "You're a much better player now, regardless of the powers. Because we've used your speed to put you in the right position, you've been able to focus on hitting the ball properly."

"Do you think I can beat Roger?"

"Definitely. You're ready and this is your chance. Concentrate every second, hit deep, seventy percent to his backhand, and attack the short balls."

"I'll make sure my excellent coach gets a share of the winnings."

"There aren't any."

"A pint, then."

*****

Paul had a spare hour before meeting Sarah for lunch, and Rob borrowed him for two tasks. First came some fine-tuning of their villain-battling routine. They practised behind the hedge bordering the courts, as far out of view as possible. They developed a new routine with a layer of misdirection built in. Triggered by the code word "wrong", confusing in itself, it worked like this: assuming Paul initiated the routine, he'd shout "wrong" and deliberately draw attention to a particular area or direction, and then the real action would take place in the opposite direction. Simple in principle, but the complication lay in exactly what the real action was that Paul would instigate. Rob would need to rapidly deduce this from Paul's manner and movements, and react accordingly. They tried out several scenarios, mostly involving dealing with multiple attackers.

Afterwards, they walked into town towards Paul's lunch date. A diversion to Upper Brook Street and the *Hampshire Chronicle* offices set up the second task. On the way, Rob offered some names for Paul's efficiency software.

"How about Culture Shock? Symbolizes a new and fun culture is needed to achieve efficiency savings."

"Hmmm, not bad."

"Or Zwoot? Snappy and the sound of an efficiency improvement flying past."

"Um."

"Or Zwump?"

They arrived at the *Hampshire Chronicle*. Rob pointed out it was one of England's oldest publications, first published in 1772—and in fact, for nigh-on two hundred years, printing took place at its base in Winchester High Street, a building reportedly haunted by a lady ghost clanking the machinery of a bygone printing press. Paul knocked and opened the door.

A fiftyish man raised his head from a PC screen. Tall and fit-looking, jeans and a jumper—Saturday attire. He turned out to be George, manning the advertising desk.

"Can we speak to one of your correspondents, Jerome Laroche?" Paul said.

"Funny you should ask," George said. "He's based at our head offices in Staple Gardens." He turned to a woman standing to his right, fingers typing a rapid text message. "But Rebecca was there earlier and he quit this morning, didn't he?"

Rebecca was younger, late twenties. Also smarter-dressed, a skirt suit. Light brown hair, to the shoulders. She finished texting before answering George. "Yes, he apologised and resigned for personal reasons. He promised to send one last article." She shifted focus to Paul and Rob, mainly Paul. "He was only with us on secondment but had another six weeks to go. A shame, he gave us a charming, Gallic flavour." She smiled. "Can I help you?"

Paul asked where to find Jerome but she didn't know. He'd mentioned some travel before returning to Bordeaux and said he'd stay in touch. She and most of the office were taken with him, and she sketched a quick picture: outgoing and livening the office up, sharing quirky theories on the British and on journalism; didn't appear to take the Velvet Vandal seriously, except as source for a story arc, though maybe knew more than he let on; no steady girlfriend, but a mystery woman who "captivated his heart".

Rob asked who would report on the Velvet Vandal now. She thought that would be her and if they found any information from Jerome or elsewhere, please get in touch. Paul took her business card and they said goodbye and left.

Outside the *Chronicle*, they confirmed a time to meet at the Cathedral. Paul headed to the top end of the High Street. Rob decided to get a snack, perhaps something from one of the market stalls.

*****

Kings Worthy proved to be a dead end and could be eliminated from the search. No five-metre Round Tables, no rickety outbuildings adapted for illicit purposes, no suspicious activities noticed by the residents—other than his own questioning about flying figures and the like. Rob had searched the area by a combination of driving along the roads and lanes, racing on foot from building to building, and a bit of cautious flying over the rural areas. He wore his active clothing: trail trainers, black hiking trousers and light blue long-sleeved top. Practical and kind of smart.

He flew low against a hedge and landed in some isolated farmland to mark the end of the search. He removed his mask and started to run back to the car, three miles away. It came on within seconds. A heaviness filled his legs. Fatigue coursed through his body. He tried to accelerate to test his speed—he couldn't. His top speed was no faster than a normal sprint. His powers were gone. Panic hit him. He breathed. Tested a few things. Vision: still good. Strength: try a one-armed press-up— just about, but hard work. He rested, one knee to the ground. Then his mind attacked: He wasn't going to find the hideout or beat the Velvet Vandal or the professor. Worse than that, he'd wasted these powers and now they were going or gone. His friends had all helped so much, without him reciprocating. His dreams started to disappear. He'd be better focusing on his job—making sure he kept it, seeing if it was possible to find a girlfriend, hoping his injuries didn't come back. He stood and started walking, thoughts cycling round and round. Five minutes and the legs felt a bit lighter. He pushed to a jog. He didn't notice the surroundings. Another five minutes and the energy started to return. He tried a few sprints—faster now. The fog in his brain began to shift. An all-out sprint, a quick check he was alone and he took off, flew low to the ground, threw in some twists and turns, and skidded to land next to a stile. Yes!

He jogged back to the car outside the Cart and Horses pub. Euphoria filled him, in black-and-white contrast to his earlier mood. His powers remained and he determined to make the best of them. Crucially, though, a confidence returned. You didn't need superpowers to achieve things, and he hung on to that—just in case. The black mood concerned him—only lasting fifteen minutes, but he'd never experienced anything like that. The sensation of squandering the powers particularly stayed with him. He decided to ask his friends for help.

The time approached four. Marianne should be on watch shortly. He pulled up the rota on his phone to work out when to tackle the final south west section of Winchester. It looked like this: Marianne at four o'clock, Kate at five, Paul at six, Rob at seven, Paul and Kate from eight to ten, and all of them after ten. He decided to execute the search in two phases: on the ground between five and seven, take an hour's break for his Cathedral shift, then use the twilight period after eight to fly over the area without risk of detection.

*****

He drove to town, parked near the cinema and navigated the side streets to emerge in The Square next to the City Museum. Opposite him, a tree-lined walkway led to the Cathedral and he walked towards the front entrance. The sky was clear now and a number of people were enjoying the sunshine. A game of frisbee progressed in the open space on the left, a small dog either helping or hindering. Marianne sat on a bench near the War Memorial, coffee in hand. She wore jeans and a grey fleece, unzipped.

"Hey," he said. "Anything happening?"

Nothing was. He stayed standing, hands in his pockets, and they chatted a bit. He asked the question he needed to.

"Marianne, these adventures and my changes are down to your dedicated research—and the crazy things you did in your cellar. How can I help you in return and make the most of these powers?"

"You already have. You got my samples back—which will change history." Rob wasn't sure if she was joking. "You're trying to achieve things, even if your choices are…eccentric—which is all any of us do. And you stayed friendly after I—"

"Dumped me?"

"Yeah."

"Why did you do that, by the way?"

"Sometimes we just know, Rob. Looking at life today, don't you think it's worked for the best?"

He hesitated and scuffed the ground with his feet. "Yeah."

He joined her on the bench. They both scanned the area around the Cathedral, not noticing anything out the ordinary.

"And by the way—thanks," Marianne said. "I know what I have to do now."

Rob turned and regarded her. "Any chance you're keeping

secrets from me, Marianne? Relating to the superpower formula or Jerome or…."

"Possibly," she said.

Kate arrived in running gear, slowing to a halt by the bench. She slapped hands with Marianne in a kind of high five and they chatted a bit, ignoring Rob, before Marianne left. Kate stood in front of Rob. He noticed the tight leggings…and then the loose T-shirt and pensive expression.

"Hello," she said.

"Arnold not joining us?"

"No. I thought this was our gig: you, me, Paul, Marianne." She hesitated. "Do you ever wonder…?"

"What?"

"This isn't…no, don't worry."

She did some calf stretches and wouldn't be drawn further.

They spent five minutes touring the Cathedral grounds. Then a quick look inside, where people were getting ready for the Evensong service. Rob left to pursue his hunt for the Velvet Vandal, leaving her his question to ponder: "Doubts hit me today, Kate, that I should be doing more with these powers and I'm taking people for granted. And you've helped me such a lot. Any suggestions how I can better use them—and perhaps do something for you? Have a think."

*****

Two hours later, at seven, Rob returned to swap shifts with Paul. The sun still cast shadows and the area was still populated, but the shadows were longer and the people were moving through, purposeful rather than passing time. He saw

Paul pacing in front of the Cathedral and jogged towards him.

"Any luck with the search?" Paul said.

"No, nothing doing. I'll do a flyover of the whole area after this shift—but if that draws a blank we're stuck. But the atmosphere feels right, as if there will be a resolution. I think the Velvet Vandal is…staging a performance. He means this to play out."

"Do you think he's dangerous?"

"No. I'm not entirely sure why, but when we fought I didn't detect any malice."

"We're still running to his agenda," Paul said. He started a slow walk in the direction of the High Street and Rob followed. "To win, we need an advantage. Finding his hideout may give us one."

"Indeed," Rob said. "I also have something for your next shift—just could be useful." He handed over a small package. "Explosive smoke bombs, four of them. Got them off Amazon. Creates a powerful effect—you throw them hard to the ground."

Paul put them in his back pocket, gingerly. "Impressive," he said.

Fenced-off grassland bordered the north side of the Cathedral to their right, dotted with trees and the odd gravestone. Rob asked what had become his standard question for the day, and the answer turned out similar to Marianne's.

"You have helped me. Your leap from caution to superhero detective has inspired me and extended my ambition. I always had a strong focus on creating a business, but now I'm looking ahead to expansion and building something big over the years. Plus, to be honest, it's been terrific fun!" They'd reached the edge of the grounds and stopped. "Finally got the contract from Kelly today," Paul added. A smile formed and increased and he shook the hand Rob offered. "Also—don't mention this, of course—I wonder if, in the fairly near future…the time's right to propose to Sarah."

"Blimey."

Paul had to dash home and left with an actual, literal spring in his step. Rob smiled and started his shift.

An hour of not much happening. Except one thing. The sun lowered and a coolness spread. He patrolled the grounds every now and again, sat down other times. Someone—the verger?—locked the Cathedral and disappeared into the Close. The thing that happened was a text. From an unknown number. It said, "Tonight." He called the number, but no one answered.

Kate arrived early, ahead of Paul and the start of their joint shift. She'd changed into jeans and a slim, blue duvet jacket. The pensive expression remained. She folded her arms, smiled a little.

"Hey," Rob said. "Ok?"

"Yes," she said, nodding. "You think something will happen tonight don't you?"

"I do, because I think the Velvet Vandal is controlling this. But I agree with Jerome and Marianne, he's playing a game, this won't be serious."

"What if the Velvet Vandal isn't controlling this? What if someone or something else is?"

Rob rested a hand on her shoulder, briefly. "What were you going to say earlier, 'have I ever wondered'…?"

She gave a laugh. "I'll sound daft. I was going to say 'if this is real'."

"Um."

She put a foot in front of her, leaned into a stretch. "I didn't bring Arnold or tell him any of this because he's normal—if annoying sometimes. What we're doing is not. Aside from the superpowers themselves, it…seems like we're being led to this point."

"True," Rob said. "From a practical point, though, what else can we do? I think you have to deal with any situation as it's presented. For example, I'm not motivated at work, I try and become a detective. You're frustrated patients don't get the best outcomes, you build a collaboration of like-minded professionals. Same with the whole superpowers business. You and Paul help me, we make the best decisions we can, and before we know it, there's a supervillain, a sinister professor and we're staking the Cathedral out. Strange but real. All we can do is follow events through and see what happens."

"Unless…you know something's wrong." Kate shook herself and clapped her hands together. Her introspective mood vanished. "Which I don't. You're right Rob, we've got cases to solve and I love the adventure."

"Adventure, I promise." He pointed an arm high and forward in superhero pose. "Once the action starts, you'll almost hear the sound of stirring music strike up—imagine the Dick Barton theme tune—and then the swashbuckling will start. We'll be like Zorro, the Three Musketeers—"

"Dangermouse?"

"Exactly."

Paul turned up. "Everything under control?" he said.

Rob left them to their shift.

Chapter 22

Rob drove through St Cross, passing the BP garage and The Bell Inn on his left. The setting sun dominated his right, blue sky giving way to a spectrum of yellow, orange and red. Bruce Springsteen played on the CD, "Thunder Road". He continued driving, exploring the area he wanted to cover: up the hill to Sainsbury's and a couple of miles beyond, then looping past the golf course and through the villages of Hursley and Otterbourne, returning to St Cross.

He executed a further, smaller circuit, taking time to think. Kate's conversation *had* disturbed him a little, suggesting things may not be as they seem. His disquiet arose from a sense she held something back. However…Rob thought it more likely an intangible feeling than a deliberate omission. And to be fair, they must be missing something. The links between the Velvet Vandal, his Year of Culture, Marianne's research, and Professor Wolf's potential crime spree were far from clear. Marianne definitely had secrets and Rob just assumed she knew what she was doing.

He parked opposite the fish and chip shop at the start of Stanmore Lane. The sky had darkened enough to obscure his flying, yet retained enough light to track ground structures. Perfect.

A text from Kate beeped at him, "Hi, nothing happening so far. Excuse strange mood earlier. On your earlier question, no one would know what to do with superpowers. You've done your best and given us a brilliant summer. Nothing more is required, except…make it real, x."

Rob left the car, a spirit of cheer and optimism upon him.

He sprinted along roads and paths and up steps to a group of trees at the edge of the grassland common of Whiteshute Ridge. He planned to fly in one-minute segments to avoid any danger of his earlier fatigue, and put his mask on. Kate's positive response to his question joined those of Paul and Marianne, and skyrocketed his confidence. He suspected they were being kind, but he had their support. He wouldn't necessarily find the hideout, but he was doing his best, not wasting his powers, and their endeavours made sense. A burst of speed, an upward acceleration, an instinctive manoeuvre to avoid a branch and the open sky welcomed him.

He made a random dart to the right and one spectacular swoop—he couldn't resist—before starting the serious search. The common below consisted of a narrow strip of rural land with housing to the right and a larger wilderness on the left, which formed a triangle between St Cross, Sainsbury's and the A3090. Half-light reigned and ground-dwelling objects such as trees and houses appeared as silhouettes. A crescent moon hung in the sky and stars started to appear.

He streaked to the left and flew over the wasteland. Untamed grassland merged with wild patches of tangled undergrowth—brambles, thistles, stinging nettle beds. Trees and bushes provided a variety of height across the terrain. A narrow path led through some of the more inhospitable ground, and traversed a small dip and rise in elevation. None of these provided the standout spectacle. A series of abandoned stone and metal structures cast shapes across the landscape, crowned by a concrete square the size of a football pitch and the twisted, blue whale-sized metallic framework of a long-collapsed building.

He knew what it was: Bushfield Army Camp. He'd seen it

on the map and read a brief history. He hadn't realised the buildings still existed—albeit in a state of surrender to the elements. Bushfield had been a World War II training camp for British and American soldiers, and later used for National Service training and as a base for the Royal Green Jackets. It closed in 1965.

He landed on the cracked and weed-strewn square, which had been the parade ground. The metal skeleton of the large building faced him, well over a hundred foot long. Maybe the barracks? Waste-high vegetation surrounded most of the structure and trees grew along the far edge, obscuring and merging with the steel columns. Several bushes also managed to push through the central concrete floor. He rotated a full three-sixty degrees. Tarmac tracks criss-crossed the area and solid shapes loomed through the remaining light: another metallic shell to his right, but a third the size and with partial, ivy-covered walls still standing; a grouping of stone buildings in various states of collapse; an intact low concrete building with multiple skylights—probably the armoury. Vegetation crowded them all, but, as Rob stood alone in the twilight, enough details were visible to evoke a powerful picture of the past: soldiers joking and smoking together, firing on the range, eating in the mess tent, fixing trucks, entering and exiting the buildings around him.

Fascinating and eerie. There was no cover to hide anything like the Round Table, though, and there were no signs anyone had been here recently. Rob headed upwards and onwards, with a nervous glance behind. A shadow near the armoury caught his eye. Probably a fox.

Thirty minutes later, Rob skidded to a landing next to a barn somewhere near Compton Down. Empty farmland surrounded him. A large opening on the long side served as the doorway. A few steps and he entered, pulling a slim flashlight from one of the multiple pockets in his trousers. It didn't take long to check out: a haystack, a tired-looking tractor, and a miscellany of machinery and farming implements. No stolen culture.

He stepped outside. A mild tiredness came over him, nothing like the fatigue of earlier. He rested a few minutes. A compulsion to complete the search—about half complete—persisted. At least he'd have done everything possible to find the hideout. The urge felt analogous to exam revision, where every last section has to be learnt—even if you're still revising in the exam hall queue—or the part missed will prove crucial. Never should have failed German GCSE. Visibility would become a problem soon. Atmospheric refraction of the sun still supplied a shimmer of light, but not for much longer. An owl hooted overhead. The other option was to go with his gut and focus on one promising area. Bushfield Army Camp stuck in his mind—maybe because of that shadow, or something else subconsciously registered.

A text beeped—from his first client, Mrs Jones. "Hello Robert. My friend Natalie has disappeared. She usually lets me know so I can look after the cat. Probably no big deal but thought I'd tell you as she's excited about you working on her case. Margaret." He brushed his hands over his head. That would have to wait. He launched himself across the fields and back towards Bushfield.

The final vestiges of twilight faded as he flew over the structures of the derelict camp, but the moon and stars furnished a faint illumination. A quick search from the sky…and there was the shadow again. It had strayed from the armoury—reaching halfway to the main road—and moved slowly, scouting amongst a cluster of bushes. Rob watched for a moment…good grief, it was huge. He flew over, aiming to land a safe distance away. The urban myths of big cats loose in the countryside came to mind. Or giant anteaters. A shaggy length of course brown-grey fur with distinctive black and white marking on the throat and shoulder areas and a ridiculous snout snuffled in front of him. Apart from a quizzical look, it ignored him. Gold dust. This must be the animal stolen from Marwell Zoo. He thought that had been a juvenile—but this was over five foot long. A short length of rope, ending in some frayed fibres, attached to a collar worn by the anteater.

Rob left the animal and flew to the armoury, where he'd first seen the shadow. He found the rest of the rope in a confused mess of knots, one end tied to a tree. Hector—he remembered the name now—must have broken free. Brambles and bushes shielded the building. Despite attempts at concealment, signs of trodden and broken foliage revealed a trail to the entrance.

The time neared ten o' clock and he called Kate, said he had something and would be late, could they hang on. She said fine, nothing to report at the Cathedral, and she was helping Paul come up with a better business name. He said goodbye. What was wrong with Zwoot?

He approached the armoury entrance, pulled aside the covering debris and ducked inside. A strong animal smell hit him. His flashlight lit up man-sized areas of floor or wall wherever he pointed it. He swept the light frequently to avoid dark, unseen, and, to be honest, scary regions. Artistic and colourful graffiti decorated the walls. A second room contained straw bedding, presumably for the anteater, and a locked chest. Superpowers or not, it took ten minutes to open. In the end, he gained some leverage by jamming the chest against the doorway and threading the rope through the lock. He tugged upwards and backwards with abrupt yanks. The third tug separated the lid amongst a shower of splinters, and somersaulted the chest. Winchester's stolen culture spilled out—official bronze measuring tankards, a mass of tiles from the Roman mosaic, sleeping dog sculpture, and more. The sculpture was definitely a fox. A quick check in the final room and, behind a sturdy rectangle of wood, and well wrapped up, he found George Shaw's The Unicorn. He punched the air. Yes! Only the Round Table missing now.

He hatched a plan: take the picture with him; sort the rest of the culture tomorrow; get to the Cathedral and see what's happening; and, er…do something with the anteater.

Hector had strayed perilously close to the A3090, unfortunately near a gap in the hedge leading straight to the road. Rob stood back, wary of the claws. The anteater acted unconcerned, as if used to humans flying and landing near him. Rob tried herding from a distance by running back and forth, clapping his hands and gesturing away from the road—to no effect. He tentatively grasped the rope and pulled. Then harder. Once Hector noticed, he resisted. His claws dug in, his back arched. Rob budged him a fraction. Suddenly he stopped resisting and lumbered towards him, knocked him flat, and stood over him. Rob had nowhere to go. He took a breath and the anteater licked him. Rob tried to stand, and Hector started pushing and nudging him. Amazingly, he seemed playful. Even so, Rob wasn't getting anywhere. He should call the zoo…or police…or RSPCA. He pulled his phone out. Kate rang.

She gave a clear, succinct summary. Paul had disappeared. She'd gone for coffees and couldn't find him on her return. His phone went straight to voicemail. No one else was near the Cathedral, although a fair few people were outside the pubs in The Square, a hundred yards back. Marianne hadn't turned up, but had sent a text to say she was running late. As Kate stood by the War Memorial, a figure shot past her—faster than even Rob's six-second hundred metres. A note fluttered to the ground: "I have Paul and Marianne. Bring Culture Man, no one else. The Cathedral roof. VV."

Rob asked her to wait at The Square, he'd be right there. Asked if she could get some apples.

He looked at the anteater. They were right by the road now and the sound of traffic highlighted the danger. He needed a course of action, and quick. How about...tie Hector to that stunted tree and hope it held a few minutes, race back for the car, drive round and park next to the gap in the hedge, bundle Hector into the car, and floor it back to the Cathedral. Was that remotely feasible?

Seven minutes later he drove through St Cross with controlled speed, George Shaw's painting in the boot and a surprised anteater exploring the back seat. He diverted along St Swithun Street, passing the high city wall on the left and, at the end, the medieval Kingsgate on the right, brightly-lit print shop built into its archway. Almost eleven now and Priory Gate still stood open—a stroke of luck, he thought it was locked at ten each night. The car screeched into a deserted Cathedral Close and followed a curving road, the elm tree from which he and Paul rescued the cat off to his right. He braked to a halt side-on to the Cathedral. Lighting gave a yellow glow round the building. He leapt out the car, then reached back inside for his grey fleece—it was colder now. He raced through the adjacent passageway and up the walkway to The Square.

Kate waited at the entrance, a bag of apples in her hand. She looked good, alive.

"How did you find those?" Rob said.

"Don't ask," she said. "What possible reason—"

"I think the best plan is for me go in and you wait outside, keep in contact. You can arrange backup if anything goes wrong."

"Sure," she said, and started walking towards the Cathedral. Old-fashioned street lights ringed the frontage and shone bright to ensure it dominated the scene, everything else fading into the background.

"You think you should come in?" Rob said.

"Rob, this is what I signed up for. My friends are inside and you'll need my help." She turned partway towards him. "Besides, I can hear the Dick Barton music."

Rob paused, then a faint smile. "Fair enough."

The front doors were locked and Kate led them through the arched passageway on the right, towards Rob's car. Although lights from the historic Cathedral Close residencies did illuminate the area, this side was darker. Also quieter—not a soul within eye- or earshot. A few yards from the car, a bang sounded and then a trumpet-roar. A long mass of fur turned on the back seat, a snout appeared at the window and a black-and-white-streaked shoulder barged against it.

Kate stepped back into Rob. "What on earth...?"

"This is Hector," Rob said. "The stolen anteater from the zoo—I'll explain later."

He peered round Kate and further down the passage, one

hand still on her arm. A small side door looked fractionally ajar. "I think we're been invited in," he said.

"We can't leave Hector here," Kate said. "He's distressed."

"Yeah, I know. We have to take him with us. There's a lot of space inside. He can settle down and we'll call the RSPCA afterwards."

A swift opening of the car door, a rapid grab for the rope and a guiding tug, and an anteater stood between them, snout in the air. Kate placed an apple in front of him. After an investigative sniff, he turned it to pulp with surprisingly dextrous claws. He hoovered up all traces in seconds using an efficient flicking tongue. He pushed at Kate with his shoulder. "I think he likes you," Rob said.

They didn't know what lay ahead and, out of precaution, decided to leave word. Rob called Julie, the only person he knew familiar with the situation. She had gone away, to her parents in Wales, and was working all hours trying to finish the PhD. Rob summarised the situation. They agreed on a text or call on the hour, starting midnight, and she'd call the police if she heard nothing by ten past. She asked how his biochemistry was coming on.

The sound of a soft thud and a click carried diagonally across the Close. Rob saw a figure exiting the Deanery Cottage and gestured for Kate to duck behind the car. He scrambled to the boot-end of the car and risked repeated glances beyond, all the time keeping a tight hold on Hector's lead. A tall, fifty-something man in jeans and dark jumper—the Dean?—walked across the grass towards the houses opposite. Halfway, he stopped and stared directly at the car. Rob realised it shouldn't be here—and almost certainly would wind up locked in for the night. The man started to walk in their direction. The anteater pushed at Kate and she pushed back. The man kept walking. Rob shrugged at Kate. Even if Hector kept still and quiet, once the man reached the car and stepped either to front or rear, he would see them. Ten feet away now. Rob reinforced his grip on Hector. Kate shifted to crouch behind the bonnet, the opposite end to Rob. Five feet away and she lobbed an apple high over the man's head. It crashed through a tree and bounced on the road. The man stopped and looked back. He took another step forward, then stopped again and eventually walked away. Rob watched him retreat, from his vantage point at the rear of the car. The man paused near the apple's landing spot, continued to a house and, after waiting for the door to open, disappeared inside.

Rob gave Kate the thumbs-up and breathed a massive sigh of relief. "Let's go," he said.

Between them, they pulled Hector towards the doorway, thirty yards away. Progress was initially stop-start as Hector dug his claws in, but in the end he trotted along and they reached the entrance.

Rob pushed the door open. "Remember," he said, "the Three Musketeers."

"There's only two of us," Kate said. Hector nudged her and she shook her head.

They entered the Cathedral.

Chapter 23

Rob shut the door behind them, and they stood in the stone corridor of the south aisle. A few light sources, high on the walls, provided a half-light and created shadows of various sizes, right up to monstrous. To their left the aisle ended at the main west entrance. To the right, stone stairs could be seen in the distance. At that point, the Cathedral widened and doors led off to the three-storey South Transept, the oldest part of the Cathedral together with the opposite North Transept. The South Transept housed the Morley Library, home of the Winchester Bible, and the Cathedral museum and gallery. Past the stairs, the Cathedral stretched yet further to reinforce the sense of length: one hundred and seventy metres long, seventeen seconds for an Olympic sprinter. Ten-foot-diameter gothic columns separated the aisleway from the central nave.

They walked between two columns into what seemed a vast space. Chairs normally set out for worshippers and service-goers had been removed, creating an open expanse. The roof was higher here, eighty-odd feet. They were halfway between the imposing, oaken entrance doors and, to their right, a raised dais which led to the choir—a chapel-like area with ancient choir stalls—and then the presbytery and sanctuary. More chapels lay beyond the sanctuary and, off to the side, was the entrance to the crypt. Back to the left, above the entrance doors, was possibly the most stunning feature: the huge stained west window, spanning the width of the nave and reaching to the vaulted roof, glinting erratically in the dim light. The medieval panes had been destroyed by Cromwell's soldiers in the mid-1600s. However, the locals had gathered the glass fragments, and, twenty years later, on restoration of the monarchy, put them together randomly to produce a collage effect. The empty, reverent surroundings disposed them to silence, and Rob just pointed left. Even Hector made no noise over the stone floor, his claws curled up and walking on his knuckles.

Ledgerstones mingled with blank flagstones to form an integral part of the floor. They passed several: Richard Cockburn B.D. (Batchelor of Divinity), 1831; Anne, wife of James Earle, 1686, who died aged about twenty and "whose vertous, pious and charitable mind, pleasant conversation and discreet demeanour towards all people caused her to be both admired and beloved while living and as much lamented when dying"; Robert Crawford, 1828, aged twenty-five years. The briefest of details for lives long gone and stories lost.

Kate broke the spell. "What's that?" she said, pointing at a clutter of objects near the wall of the north aisle.

Rob led them through a second set of columns, still holding Hector's rope. A Jane Austen exhibition displayed in blue cabinets against the surrounding pillars, text and illustrations summarising her life. Her ledgerstone lay in front of them. Beyond was an open toolbox. Tools jutted from the top compartment, including screwdrivers and a mini-crowbar. A decorative, three-foot-tall brass plaque leaned against the wall. An empty recess of lighter-coloured stone showed where it should have been. The plaque's inscription had the title "Jane Austen" in large lettering. It continued with her memorial, starting with the words "known to many by her writings".

"The Velvet Vandal," Rob said, quietly. "This is priceless history and world famous. To steal this would be shocking. We need to stop him." No humour and the first time Kate had seen him angry.

"Jane Austen's memorial?" she said.

"Yes. Her ledgerstone has a memorial from the funeral in 1817, but it doesn't mention the writing. Her nephew, who was at the funeral, commissioned the plaque and it was erected in 1872. Thousands come to see it every year."

Kate gazed over the wall, above and to the left of the recess. A series of dedications and memorials caught her attention, many of a military nature: George Gosling, Captain in the Rifle Brigade, died 1906 at Niangaru, Congo state while on an exploring expedition; the "one thousand nine hundred and five British Officers, Gurkha Officers and Men of the 10th Princess May's Own Gurkha Rifles who gave their lives 1890-1994"…. "We need to find Paul and Marianne," she said.

"The note said the Cathedral roof," Rob said. "My guess would be the interior roof—maybe the ringing chamber or the bell room—rather than on top the tower itself. The Velvet Vandal tends to follow the blog, so it makes sense to retrace the route we used on the tour." He pointed at a small oak door, left of the entrance doors. "That's the way up."

Kate nodded. As they crossed back towards the nave, she stopped at Jane Austen's ledgerstone, distracted herself. "Is she actually buried here?" she said.

"Yes, her coffin's underneath—well, actually shifted about a yard to the right, something to do with when they installed central heating. There are seven hundred-odd ledgerstones in the Cathedral with bodies below, and more people are buried with no markings. They stopped burying people in churches and cathedrals mid-1800s for health reasons."

"Spooky isn't it?"

Rob dropped to one knee. He breathed hard. He let go of

the rope and the anteater shuffled into the nave, snout to floor.

"Are you all right?" Kate said.

Rob didn't reply. She moved over and crouched in front of him.

"Just need…a few minutes," he said.

Kate got him to sit against a column. She put a hand on his brow—nothing abnormal. She placed two fingers on his neck, next to the windpipe, counted his pulse against her watch.

His breathing normalized after a couple of minutes. Another minute and he looked up, gave a half-smile. "Happened this afternoon," he said. "Out of breath and then real fatigue for about fifteen minutes. My powers disappeared—couldn't sprint, couldn't fly."

Kate rechecked his pulse. "Pulse was high," she said. "Over a hundred. It's almost normal now."

Rob stood and took a few paces. "When this happened earlier, I panicked that the powers had gone. Once they returned I was good as new. I figured I'd overused them."

"What time was that?"

"About half three—eight hours ago. It felt similar to when I first got the lizard bite and the start of all this, though that lasted a day or two." He hesitated. "Also…this kind of hopelessness came over me. My mind kept drilling at me—saying I'd failed, wasted the powers, wouldn't achieve anything. I couldn't concentrate on anything."

"You don't feel that now?" Kate said.

"No. I think you've helped, and Paul and Marianne. Made me realise I may not be perfect, but I'm making an effort. This feels different: excitement about the powers returning and what I can do with them, linked with a kind of sadness that maybe they will go sometime." He glanced into her eyes. "Do you think I am losing them?"

Yes, Kate thought. She hoped there was nothing worse. "I honestly don't know, Rob." She gave him a spontaneous hug.

He tried a few sprints up and down the nave. The speed was lightning-quick as ever. He halted next to her. After a moment's recovery, he said, "All the energy's back. Although…the flying isn't there. I shied away from taking off. Didn't feel right. Probably needs a bit longer." The voice sounded flat and he put his hands in his pockets, looked at the floor.

He insisted he was fully recovered and they continued towards the tower door. Hector had lain down in the darkness of the south aisle, behind a pillar. His front paws stretched forward, head resting on them and he watched them. Kate emptied the apples in front of him. They left him there and reached the door.

It was unlocked. Rob pushed it open to reveal a narrow stone staircase and turned to face Kate. "I tell you what," he said, animation back in his voice. "In case I am losing my powers—which I'm not—we should go out in style, with a dash and a touch of flair."

She gave him a smile. "Absolutely."

Rob leapt up the first few steps and Kate followed. A little further and all light vanished. He drew the flashlight from his pocket. They climbed in silence, aside from soft footsteps sounding on smooth stone. The torch cast patches of light and semi-light on an unchanging scene, stone spiralling upwards over a hundred-plus steps. After a couple of minutes, they reached the exit door. It led outside onto the narrow ledge of the south parapet.

The nave roof sloped up to their left and stretched ahead

to reveal the dark shapes of the tower and the south transept. Eighty feet below was the Cathedral Close and beyond that the lights of the city. A couple of yards along the ledge was a door, which led them into the roof space above the nave.

"Shouldn't all these doors be locked," Kate said.

"Yes. The vergers are meant to take care of that. Looks like we're being left a trail." Rob hesitated. "I could fly along the roof—scout out the tower area and the ringing chamber." He tensed himself, tested a kind of half-leap.

"No way," Kate said. "Not till we understand what your body's doing." She stood between Rob and the door.

He only paused a second. "Yeah, of course you're right," he said. "Thanks."

Next to them was a small row of windows in the triangular end-wall, a humbler extension of the stained west window below. Light crept through, enough to see their near-surroundings. The space extended left and right for the width of the nave, terminating where the sloping roof met the floor. Ancient wooden beams crossed the area: huge horizontal ones across the full floor width; vertical posts up through the centre line to the apex twenty feet above; and smaller diagonal ones that the roof appeared to rest on. Additional connecting beams and supporting cables created a busy space. A central wooden walkway, railings to either side, led into the gloom-filled interior. Rob's torch light dispersed into darkness long before finding an endpoint. A small scrabbling noise sounded somewhere ahead.

"This really is spooky," Rob said.

Kate agreed and all of a sudden it seemed more serious. She located a light switch. They decided not to use it and started along the walkway, as noiseless as possible. Concrete and brick-walled pits were to either side. They were about twelve foot deep and contained a loose scattering of rubble. A shape flitted in front of them. The environment—time-worn beams, steep pits and darkness—stayed constant, aside the occasional bat. Kate soundlessly tapped the railings every few steps. A full two minutes and Rob's torch picked out a stone wall in front of them. A narrow gap led down six or seven stairs to a door. They slowed and Rob shielded the torch. At the top of the stairs, they saw light under the door and stopped. A sound penetrated. A creak. Then another. Nothing for a while. A murmur—a voice.

Rob motioned backwards. They retreated about twenty paces and spoke in low voices.

"That's the ringing chamber," Rob said. "It's a square room, quite large. About twelve metres by twelve."

Kate folded her arms, pursed her lips. What now? "Any other way in?" she said.

"One other. There's a second stairway by the south transept. That leads to a similar door to this one—on the opposite side of the room, in the right hand corner." He pointed. "If you carry further up the stairway you get to the bell room and eventually the tower roof."

"So the setup the other side is basically the same as this." Kate said. "If we're going in, this door is as good as any." She leaned on the railings. Thick beams below her extended across one of the pits. Rob's light played across them to give a whitish, ghost-like hue. "We need a plan."

"I was afraid it would come to that," Rob said.

Kate smiled. Tension relieved, to a point. "We could knock."

"Not a terrible idea," Rob said. "There's no way to get in

undetected, anyway. I still can't get away from thinking this is some kind of game. Maybe I'm wrong." He joined her on the railings. "At least we should take advantage of there being two of us."

Kate turned her head. She noticed him staring into the distance, thoughtful. One arm on the rail, one hand in pocket, fleece open, dark hair covering half his forehead…some curl at the end. Their elbows were touching. "Anything in the room that might help us?" she said, softly.

Rob mentioned a couple of things. A trapdoor in the centre of the floor opened above the presbytery, eighty feet below, and was mirrored by one from the bell room in the ceiling above. They were used to lower the bells for maintenance but hadn't been used since 1937. Would be hard to open and much too dangerous to play with. The clock mechanism was up some steps in a wooden hut on the right side of the room. The clock struck on the quarter hour using a chime called ting-tang—one high note, one low—with one sequence sounding on the first quarter, two on the half hour, up to four for the full hour. The hour would also strike, so at midnight there would be twenty strikes—four tings, four tangs and twelve hour strikes.

The time was almost quarter to midnight. They decided Rob would go in and rapidly assess. Kate would react depending on circumstances. They discussed several scenarios, including Rob luring the Velvet Vandal away for Kate to enter the room.

They moved silently to the top of the stairs leading to the door. Kate concealed herself in the darkness behind the wall. The clock struck the first ting-tang, slightly late. Rob gave a thumbs-up. Kate returned the gesture, but he'd already accelerated down the steps.

CULTURE MAN

*****

Rob charged the door open. He came to an instant stop the other side, weight on his toes, muscles tense, ready to react. He adjusted to the light and scanned the room before the second chime faded. Most of the details were as he remembered: a large, uncluttered space with twenty-foot-high ceiling; bell ropes hanging down to about ten feet; cold stone walls— gothic pillars alternating with regular stone; plaques and pictures on the walls; wooden hut to the right; two swords in a glass case, high on the wall behind him; a few narrow windows, well above head-height and covered with black cloth. Paul and Marianne were tied to chairs in front of him, three-quarters the way across the room. The Velvet Vandal reclined on a chair halfway along the left wall, hands behind his head and feet resting on a wooden box. The third and final chime sounded.

The Velvet Vandal wore his uniform of charcoal cape and hood, black mask and black leggings with dark shiny stripes above the knee. Black suede boots finished the effect, to the ankle and slightly pointed. He spoke in a clearer voice than Rob remembered. He still couldn't place the accent. "We meet again, Culture Man."

"For goodness sake," Rob said. "Did you rehearse that?"

"No. I'm having fun. You took your time."

"I've been clearing out your hideout," Rob said. "Bushfield Camp."

The Velvet Vandal flexed his feet, pointing the toes forward. "A fascinating place, no?"

Rob focussed on Paul and Marianne. Rope wrapped around

their torsos, binding their arms to their sides and fastening them to the chairs. Their legs were tied together. They could move their feet from side to side, to an extent. "You both ok?" he said.

"Physically fine," Paul said, sounding calm. "No one else is here. This guy's strong."

Marianne nodded. "Fine, except annoyed," she said, and sounded it. "This is stupid." She glared at the Velvet Vandal. "He's at maximum strength now, but it won't last—"

Rob exploded from his front calf and streaked to the side of the chairs. An instant change of direction and he was behind Paul and Marianne, reaching for the knot securing Paul. The Velvet Vandal was already there, catching his arms, twisting him in a half-circle and pushing him back to the centre of the room. Much stronger than before. A shove sent him staggering back. He rolled and came up in a crouch.

The Velvet Vandal held his hand up. "Wait," he said. "This is not necessary."

Rob nodded, saw his opponent relax and dived at him. He brought him down. They rolled on the floor, grasped at each other, searched for a solid hold. Somehow he needed to negate the superior strength. Keep moving—try and use the Velvet Vandal's own momentum against him. He had some success. Left arm round his shoulder and right round his waist, he kept rolling, measured the distance so the next roll slammed the Velvet Vandal into the side wall. Rob jumped to an almost standing position. Paul shouted a warning, but too late and a foot behind his knee wrenched him down. There was motion behind him. The door had opened and Kate sprinted for the chairs. She tackled the knot behind Paul.

The Velvet Vandal manoeuvred to face the back of the

room. He grabbed Rob with an increasingly tight hold on his fleece. He jammed a foot against a pillar. Rob couldn't move him at all and felt himself pulled in an arc towards and over the Velvet Vandal. The force ratcheted and he could only hold out a couple of seconds. He lost grip and grabbed at the hood. He tore it before he was sent flying to the front of the room and crashed against the wall. The Velvet Vandal leapt up, waves of dark hair showing. In a blur of motion, he was at Kate's side and scooped her up by the waist. She struggled but to no effect. A couple of long strides and he dumped her to the right of Rob. He strode back to his chair on the left wall.

Rob stood. His shoulder hurt, but only a bruise. He checked Kate. She gave a rueful look and a thumbs-up. He stayed alert and watchful, but took a breather, waited for the next move.

"Please," the Velvet Vandal said. "We should discuss. We're on the same side."

Rob looked at Paul and Marianne.

"There are some things you should hear," Marianne said.

"Ok," he said.

"Do you know who he is?" Paul said.

The Velvet Vandal ripped off the remainder of his hood, and then the mask. "I won't need this anymore." He undid the front of the cape to reveal a grey polo neck. He stood with hands behind his back and surveyed the room. Mid-thirties. Full hair—in casual disarray at the front, somehow still neat. Touch of stubble meeting sideburns. Brooding look, but combined with a twinkle in the eyes. "Bonjour," he said.

So, not Arnold or Roger, then. "Jerome Laroche," Rob said.

"No less." He addressed Kate. "I am sorry for manhandling you. You're Kate, I think?"

"Hi," she said.

Marianne cleared her throat.

"Ah yes, and sorry for tying you up, Marianne."

Marianne said, "There are important things to—"

"We're not on the same side," Rob said. "And I won't let you take the Jane Austen memorial. Why are you stealing culture from my blog?"

Jerome paced a couple of steps. "It is not personal."

Rob noticed Paul twisting his hands behind the chair. Hopefully Kate had loosened the rope.

He switched subject, trying to distract. "Why aren't you speaking in your eccentric English? Where are the 'incidents of high seriousness', the 'no longer can we be shocked', the 'be aware that I will keep you informed'?"

Jerome laughed. "I'm honoured you follow my work. I'm a professional journalist and can write in perfect and boring English if I wish. But I've created a persona, something exotic, to give my readers an experience."

"Fair enough," Paul said. "I bet he's more you than you admit, though."

"About the culture?" Rob said.

"I shall tell you. The reason is the story. Journalists love to tell a story, but there is more: we can shape a tale, even create one. Study the elements here." Jerome ticked items off on his fingers. "Ancient history, high art, popular culture, a mystery masked man threatening them all, an impossible theft…and then an adversary and a thrilling climax. The stakes are raised: Jane Austen's memorial stolen—or maybe not. No matter, she captivates all and the world will read the story."

"You'll be in prison," Rob said.

"That is…one possibility. I'm not really a vandal. The treasure is safe and merely needs to be found. All my incidents tell their own tale. Imagine the Round Table in years to come. People will say it's hung in the Great Hall for centuries, apart from the Velvet Vandal episode. I have given a story for the summer and added to the history."

"You created the Velvet Vandal just to tell a story?"

"It wasn't my plan to start. But like everyone, I have my own motivations and things fell into place."

Rob stepped forward. "What of the memorial? Jane Austen doesn't need your embellishments."

Jerome hesitated. "Perhaps not, but all stories advance. It is down to you to save the memorial."

Kate stepped next to Rob. "You haven't created this story," she said. "This was real without you. Rob's blog, Marianne's research, the professor's involvement, Rob's powers, hundreds of years of history…."

"You're right—I have but added a layer and drawn some attention." Jerome regarded her. "You feel it too, don't you? A questioning of events: how can this be? This cannot be the true picture?" A twitch of her lip, and he continued. "I think you are right and wrong. I also sense we miss something, but we never understand all. Strange things happen and this is our opportunity. For me—a story to write. For you…." He shrugged.

"Some of us need to understand," Kate said. "But…we should embrace the canvas in front of us."

Jerome nodded and she seemed satisfied, in a way.

Rob returned to the narrative. "Your account makes no sense. Why pick on my blog?"

Marianne broke in. "There's something more important to

talk about," she said.

"You knew about Jerome?"

Marianne's eyes shifted to Jerome for a moment. Her tongue brushed her lip. "Some. The rest…only today."

"I want to hear Jerome's answer," Rob said.

"You were with Marianne a while," he said. "That's how I found your blog and why I started, with the oil painting. Later, I realise I have a great story."

"It still doesn't make sense."

Jerome shrugged. "I am in love with Marianne."

They all looked at him. Marianne rolled her eyes.

Silence, then Kate said, "He's quite handsome, Marianne."

Rob looked at her.

Jerome cupped his chin in his hand, tapped his fingers against his cheek. He managed to look both intense and embarrassed. "Marianne is right," he said. "There are other things to discuss."

"Let me tell this," Marianne said. "What time is it, Rob?"

"Six minutes to midnight."

Marianne nodded. She started dispassionately, as if delivering a scientific briefing—apart from being tied up. "Professor Wolf pursued research into biochemical mechanisms that could lead to aggressive cellular repair. He found more though—the potential for hyper-efficiency, or superpowers as we've called them. He became stuck and recruited me, probably because I hit on a lucky piece of research—"

"Not quite," Jerome said. "He noticed you before. Asked me to make contact, in Bordeaux. That's the first time I saw you. I think he guided you in this direction—perhaps sent some anonymous information to stir your appetite."

Marianne paused, scrunched her face. "Maybe when…." She kept focus and carried on. "He used my work to create a formula for Jerome. The result was the Velvet Vandal. His powers aren't stable and they'll run out, I'm not sure when. I think his version of the drug heightens impulses, which could explain his ludicrous behaviour."

Jerome opened his mouth. But he didn't say anything, just swept his cape round.

"I don't understand the professor's end goals but he became more demanding. Then Rob developed the powers we all know about. Once I found out about the lizard bite, I managed to synthesize a drug. A couple of problems though. First, I have a sample—the one you retrieved from Oxford—that should give long term and stable effects, but I can't repeat it. In fact I had to make some changes: a complex merging of the two samples, which the professor won't be aware of. Second, Jerome"—again she glared at him—"was working for the professor and stole my samples, and hence your epic trip to Oxford."

"I enjoyed that," Paul said.

The attention centred on Jerome and he studied the floor. "I am sorry Marianne, it's to my regret. I worked with Professor Wolf to pay a debt for my mother. I can say no more of that. The professor was exciting and driven, but a darkness crept through and he goes too far. I was not comfortable with the theft. Tonight is my final payment."

"What exactly is that?" Rob said.

"The professor wants to talk to you all. He means to negotiate with Marianne. I am to bring you to a private place. I added a touch of style with the Cathedral."

"You didn't have to tie us up," Marianne said. She struggled against the rope.

"It is a matter of honour. I promised to do so."

"Sod your honour."

"No matter," Jerome said. "Once the professor arrives, my debt is paid and I am on your side as agreed. I will release you." He turned to Rob. "We may require to work together. I hope not, but there is a chance he brings a man—short and powerful, like a bouncer. I don't know who he is, but the professor is wary of him."

"Why should we trust you?" Rob said.

"I am a man of honour."

"How can we know that?" Rob said. "All the evidence suggests not."

Jerome pulled out his mobile, pressed some buttons. "I shall reveal where the Round Table is." He showed Rob a picture.

Rob's eyes widened and he gave a short laugh. "Brilliant. I'd never have found…."

Jerome forwarded the picture to Rob's phone, then offered his hand. Rob hesitated, glanced round at his friends. Kate nodded first, then Paul. Marianne sighed, but also nodded. They shook.

"What time does the professor get here?" Kate said.

"He said midnight."

Midnight was a couple of minutes away and they fell silent.

Rob remembered to check in with Julie and sent a quick text. He adjusted the arrangement.

Rob motioned Kate and they moved into the centre of the room, away from the door. Kate paced to the right and rested her back against the hut. Jerome was on the opposite side of the room, leaning forward on his chair.

Rob put his hands in his pockets. "Jerome," he said, "after this, what will you do with your powers?"

"I shall look for a new story. One where I am the good guy, I think." A smile. "And, um, Marianne…." She gave no reaction. "Perhaps travel, somewhere exotic. And you?"

"I have a detective agency to start up. Also, some professionals take sabbaticals in the developing world, like doctors doing cataract operations. I'd like to do the same kind of thing—take the odd time out and use my powers to…improve lives." He added, casually, "A bit of exploring on the side."

Kate cleared her throat. "Guys," she said. "Remember what we discussed about Professor Wolf." She waited for their attention and added, "Probably psychopathic."

Ting-tang. The clock mechanism in the wooden hut kicked in. A set of levers led to the bells in the room above and the sound reverberated. Three more chimes marked the fourth quarter, and then twelve strikes and midnight had struck.

*****

They barely saw him enter. As the last strike faded, Professor Wolf stood in front of them. Dark navy jeans, slim with wide belt. Black polo neck jumper. Grey jacket, buttons undone. Right hand in jeans pocket. A couple of steps in front of the door. In the corner to his right, a stocky man had also intruded. Presumably Jerome's 'bouncer'—hands behind his back, wearing a suit and tie, and looking impassively ahead.

"Thank you, Jerome," Professor Wolf said. "A garage or hotel room would've been fine, but your sense of drama is impeccable." Starting with Marianne, he made eye contact with each of them. "We have much to discuss."

"You think so," Marianne said. She strained in her chair. "How about a damn big apology to start with."

The professor stayed relaxed. "There's always give and take, Marianne. Without my help, you'd have achieved none of your breakthroughs. You should calculate what gives best advantage. If you listen, we can accomplish so much brilliant science."

No one had moved since his entrance. The professor and the bouncer were at the fore of the room. Jerome, Rob and Kate stood from left to right across the centre. Paul and Marianne were tied at the back, Paul on the left.

"We're not listening to anything," Rob said.

"Our resident superhero," the professor said. "Playing out an amusing duel with Jerome. But you will listen."

"Why should we?" Paul said. "We've already taken the samples from your lab."

A light clench of his fist, scarcely noticeable. "That wasn't important—although annoying. You've earned my respect and make interesting adversaries. Which is all the more reason to hear—"

"Which we're still not interested in," Rob said.

A smile played on the professor's lips. "You're surprised to see me here. You expect me to be out stealing the crown jewels? Learning my trade as a master criminal?"

"Yes," Paul said, with surprising certainty. "Superpowers, a reckless challenge, overconfidence, the file I found. What else are you going to do?"

"The file is nothing. Created by my students, an exercise I gave them." He scanned the room, settled his gaze on Kate. "Where are my manners? We haven't been introduced.

Delighted to meet you, Kate. Your physio practise is highly recommended, as is the website. You too could help our scientific progress."

Kate didn't react.

Rob noticed a signal from the bouncer towards the professor, a small hand gesture. Impatience, maybe. Who was in charge here?

Rob walked towards Paul and Marianne. "Whatever we discuss, I'm untying my friends."

"No," the professor said. His voice rang out as a command.

Jerome removed his hands from the chair. He put them behind his back, stepped casually into the room. "It is only fair," he said. "If we are to come to an agreement, then all should be under equal conditions."

Rob knelt behind Marianne, one knee to the floor, and started to untie her.

The professor snapped his fingers. "Jerome, I need to be in control. We'll discuss later. Stop him."

"No. Our agreement is concluded and my debt is over. There is no need for this."

The professor removed his hand from his trouser pocket and reached to the inside of his jacket. He drew a gun. Pointed it at Rob.

The whole room froze.

"Move away," he said. He shifted the gun towards Kate, back to Rob. Rob stepped away.

Paul spoke first. "You've made this a whole lot more serious. How do you expect to get away with this?"

"There's a lot at stake," the professor said, "and you've been playing. Which is your mistake."

"We've been doing what's right," Rob said. "Paul's correct,

you can't possibly get away with any shooting."

The professor gave a broad smile. He lowered his arm and pointed the gun at the floor. Put his other hand in his pocket, less threatening. He stayed watchful. "This isn't a big deal. You've committed crimes against me. We're having a chat." He shrugged and scanned the room. "Jerome, your power's fading this second—until the next time. Rob, your powers will be gone soon. Both are fixable. Marianne, we can advance medicine beyond your dreams. Paul, Kate, I can provide the contacts and technology to advance your businesses. There are riches too, if you care."

"Riches are your motivation?" Rob said.

"No. But a welcome side effect. Do you know what charismatic professors are paid? We're not buying yachts."

"What do you want, Mark?" Marianne said.

"Information first," he said. "Then we can decide how to work together."

"Go on."

Everyone else stayed where they were, and the professor took the floor, pacing back and forward a little, gesticulating sometimes. Rob kept his eye on the gun. He was at the back of the room now, too far away to think of making a move.

"The mice are back to normal," the professor said.

"Really?" Marianne said.

"I thought we had a solution. Based on your notes and the initial reaction, the effects should have held. Why didn't they?"

"I'm not sure. They tailed off. Probably related to the impurities, which play a role in the early stages."

"Do you know how to fix it?"

A purse of the lips and a glance at the gun. "Consider the two examples where the effects are long-lasting." She nodded at Jerome and Rob. "Their powers have flaws, but if you compare and contrast there should be a way to obtain the long-term effect and preserve my improved version."

"Have you done that?"

"I've had a go."

"Where are the updated samples, Marianne?" The professor was on edge—back foot raised on toes as if time had stopped, excitement in his voice.

"I don't have them." The professor opened his mouth and she hurried on. "But that's not important. We still can't reproduce the formula."

The professor blew his breath out. "We will be able to. Here's the deal. I can't be traced back to any of this, and I'll find a solution in the end. But quicker and better if we work together. I want you working with me. You'll be given lab access, high salary. We'll achieve extraordinary advances. Otherwise you'll disappear into obscurity and wonder what could have been."

Marianne hesitated.

Rob interrupted. "You need to be straight with us. What's your end game? You said your plans are more ambitious than we can imagine."

"You need to understand that doesn't matter," the professor said. "The journey's the important thing. Any scientific research has beneficial spin-offs. Research into robotics leads to better artificial limbs. GPS was a pure military development and now it's ubiquitous. Rocket engine research led to a lifesaving heart pump for patients on the transplant list. There are a myriad of examples."

"We need assurance you're not...building a doomsday weapon, for instance."

The professor laughed. "I'm not the evil genius of your imagination. If you really want to know…." He turned to his right, and the bouncer gave a short nod.

"Yes?" Rob said, as the pause lengthened.

The professor looked straight ahead and said, "Immortality."

Silence a moment, until Paul said, "That's insane."

Jerome said, "It is true, it's his passion."

Marianne said, "How would you approach that? Use our mopping-up operations to extend cell life—for ever?"

"For another day," the professor said. "I don't mean immortality as in millions of years, I mean significant prolongation of life. Anti-ageing research has been around a long time—mice can live up to fifty percent longer—and our work can jump on that. If we can stop people dying, the moral imperative is to do so. I've been frank with you—"

"Not yet," Rob said. "Who's the shop floor dummy?" He nodded towards the bouncer.

Jerome caught Rob's eye, pushed his palms down, warning him. The bouncer flicked his gaze to Rob, otherwise remained impassive.

The professor seemed amused—a twitch at the corner of his mouth—but said, "You should be more polite." A short silence, then he continued. "He represents my clients. They provide funding and share a passion for the kind of science we're doing. And yes, they have their own motivation. Long life and certain powers are in their interest, but the research benefits everyone." He refocused on Marianne. "Time's passing. Marianne, let's make this deal."

Marianne pushed against the ropes, looked directly at Professor Wolf. "No," she said. "I can't trust you. I'm grateful for the experience working with you, but now's the time to leave this behind us and go separate ways. I'm sure you'll reach your goals, but remember science works by collaboration these days, not in secret."

Rob watched, full concentration. Apart from brandishing a gun, the professor had been reasonable, even charming as he tried to persuade Marianne. What when he didn't get his way?

The professor gave a shake of the head, and a mock-disappointed "Marianne." The bouncer signalled him again, definitely impatient. "You're right, collaboration builds the future, but the world isn't ready for immortality or superpowers. We need control. I'm offering you a great prize"—his voice hardened—"but if you won't take the carrot, there are sticks I can use." He advanced a pace.

Jerome matched his movement, stepped forward himself. "No," he said. "You made an offer, she says no. She's graceful and wishes you luck. Time to end this, make a new plan."

Rob tensed. He sensed action was close. At the edge of his hearing, he detected a faint scratch—somewhere the other side of the door, along the darkened walkway.

Marianne strained at the ropes again. The professor stared as she tensed her muscles. He suddenly clicked his fingers. "I understand now," he said. "You're testing your strength, not the rope. That's why you can't produce the sample. You used it on yourself and you're waiting for the powers to appear."

Marianne said nothing.

The professor continued. "That changes your bargaining power. I can take a blood sample, analyse—"

"No," Jerome said, again.

Rob edged forward. Still behind Paul and Marianne's chairs, but within touching distance. He heard another couple of scratches, closer to the door.

The professor faced Jerome. "You've forgotten your roots," he said. "Your mother would be disappointed."

"Never. She taught me honour." Jerome stiffened, his casual manner vanished. "She felt gratitude but trusted people too far. What you did was for your own—"

The scratching increased and became obvious. A bang shook the door behind the professor. It crashed open and a long, grey shape, flashes of black and white, clattered against the floor and lumbered into the room.

"Hector!" Jerome said.

Everyone stared. The professor had to turn backwards and Jerome took his chance. Slower than before, but still devastatingly quick, he was upon the professor before he could react. He reached for the gun, knocked it. The bouncer was, somehow, equally quick. He grappled Jerome and threw him forcefully against the wall. A crack sounded as his head hit. The gun fired. The bullet ricocheted off walls and Kate went down. Jerome slumped to the floor, didn't move. Rob vaulted the chairs, reached Kate in an instant and knelt beside her.

*****

She lay on her side and clutched her left arm. Grimaced. Rob gently moved her hand. A centimetre-wide hole, frayed round the edges, penetrated her jacket above the elbow. The surrounding area was damp and dark.

"How do you feel?" Rob said. "Stupid question, I know?"

"Not…terrible," she said. "Feels…numb. But stinging, burning as well."

Marianne spoke. "Rob, you need to expose the arm and

check the bleeding."

Rob eased her arm from the duvet jacket. At the corner of his attention, the professor and the bouncer conferred in low voices. The anteater had lain down at the front of the hut, not far from them. Blood coated Kate's arm from the elbow to the top of the bicep. A steady flow increased the volume.

"It's not spurting," Marianne said. "That's good, it hasn't hit the brachial artery. You need to apply pressure."

Rob cast around for something to use. He darted to the opposite side of the room to retrieve Jerome's hood and tore it into a long strip. Under Marianne's guidance, he wrapped it around Kate's arm, tied a knot—not too tight, and pressed with his hand. "Might be lucky," he said. "Looks more of a flesh wound, though I can't tell if there's an exit wound. The ricochet must have slowed the bullet." He rested his other hand on her forehead.

"I'll need to find a decent physio," Kate said. A weak smile. "I can hold the bandage."

Rob placed her hand in position, made her squeeze tight. He turned to the front. The ongoing discussion contained few words, but there was clear conflict and a tension infused the two men. The bouncer stalked back to his post in the corner. He faced the room and resumed his impassive stare.

"Someone check Jerome," Marianne said. "Mark."

The professor didn't move.

"We need to call for medical help," Paul said. "Rob."

Rob pulled out his phone.

For the first time, or at least the first time audibly, the bouncer spoke. Clearly not a bouncer, and answering the question as to who was in charge. "This has gone too far," he said. The voice was deep, limited variation in tone. He directed his words at the professor. "Finish it."

The professor hesitated. He started to raise the gun. Rob stood and positioned himself between the professor and Kate. Facing forward, Rob was on the left and half a room from the professor, on a diagonal line to his central position at the front. Too far to rush him, and the bouncer was lethal anyway. Hector lay a few feet in front of him and the bouncer further ahead, and to the professor's right. He felt the professor was trying to make a decision.

"Don't do it," Rob said.

The professor replied with a cryptic "Prepare yourself" and further hesitation. Was he going to shoot them? Planning to turn on the bouncer? Rob had no idea, but sensed an extra tension in the bouncer. Either way, he couldn't leave it to chance. What to do though?

He turned, looked at Paul and Marianne behind him, and Kate next to him. The gun pointed straight at him now. He wanted to delay, time to think, but a culpability settled upon him. He'd led them into this. "I'm sorry," he said. "This is my fault."

"Wrong," Paul said, his voice loud and clear.

A split second in his head and Rob remembered their routine. Paul slammed his feet on the wooden floor, to his right. Everyone else looked to that side. Rob focused on the left, not knowing what to expect, but ready for…something.

Paul drew a huge breath and catapulted himself and the chair forward and left in an explosive movement. He landed on his knees and rolled. The chair hit the floor side-on with a crash, kept rolling and then Paul was on top of it. The momentum let him roll one more time, and as he did so, his hands reached into his back pocket—he'd worked them free enough to give some flexibility. His fingers flicked some ball bearing-type objects into the room before he jolted to a halt, facing forward, the chair tied behind him.

Half a second had passed. The professor swung the gun back towards Rob. The bouncer twisted back towards the centre, lifted his right foot, and readied for an explosive thrust from the left calf. Rob recognised the smoke bombs he'd given Paul. Three were in motion. One scuttered off to the right. The other two bounced ahead. Rob brought every sinew into play, lunged rather than sprinted, but the speed was still there. All his concentration focused on the objects, the bouncing and skidding making the motion impossible to predict. The rightmost one kicked high off some grit or dirt and he leapt and stamped down on it, a few feet in front of the professor. An instant explosion and smoke surged forth in a spiralling whirlwind. A leap to the left and he stretched and caught the other one—another explosion and more smoke—and landed in a crouch. The bombs acted faster than he could have hoped and the room was impenetrable murk. Dark blue smoke from one merged with red from the other to create a purple shroud...maybe magenta.

A hissing noise, half-growl, came from Hector, and then a heavy padding as he ran—Rob couldn't tell which direction. Rob twisted and launched himself in the direction of the door, trying to avoid the bouncer and tackle the professor. He barged the professor in the left torso, spun and struck a downward blow where he thought the gun was. Gold dust, the gun slammed to the floor. The professor disappeared from reach. Rob swept the floor with his foot, sidefooted the gun to the back of the room. He turned to anticipate an imminent assault from the bouncer, but it didn't come. Rob felt a motion past his knee. He heard a thud to his right, rapidly followed by a yell, the clatter of something falling to the floor and a violent hissing. The bouncer must have tripped over Hector. Then a scuffling sound and a piercing cry. The commotion ended with low moaning and further rapid padding.

The activity near him ceased. His senses caught up and he felt an irritation of the throat and a sting of the eyes. He couldn't relax, there was no knowing where the advantage would unfold. He needed a weapon. A glint penetrated the smoke from high on the wall, and he remembered the swords. He accelerated upwards, half-flying. The flying worked, but seemed…harder than usual. He grasped the sword case, resting his feet against the wall. A sharp wrench, and the display crashed to the floor, glass shattering. Landing softly, he seized one sword, couldn't locate the other. He headed to the centre of the room and kept his senses keen, ready to react.

The smoke was clearing and he waited it out. The scene gradually came into focus. Marianne and Paul were still tied to chairs: Marianne unmoved and near the back, and Paul on his side about eight feet in front of her. Both faced towards the entrance door. Jerome lay haphazard on his side, to the right of the door and roughly facing the back of the room. His eyes were closed. Rob thought he could detect a rise of the chest. Hector had slumped in the back corner, snout forward, to Marianne's right—as far from the action as possible. The bouncer was front left and struggling to his feet. His jacket and shirt were shredded and bloodied across a diagonal line from chest to hip. The anteater must have slashed him. The blood continued to seep, turning the shirt crimson. He stepped forward, his knee buckling a little, and grimaced, but looked dangerous, capable of overriding the pain and blasting into action. Kate was sitting up, on the left of the room, a little behind Rob. Steps behind her led down to the second exit door. Her right arm hugged across her chest, allowing her wrist and forearm to press against the bandage around her left bicep. She held the gun in her right hand and it pointed at the bouncer. The professor stood to the front right, a sneer on his face, and the other sword in his hand. People set out like a chessboard.

"Jerome's breathing, Marianne," Rob said.

"Thank goodness," she said.

The bouncer lurched another step, steadier now. Kate said, voice clear, "Another move and I shoot."

The last of his grimace disappeared, and the impassive gaze returned and fixed on her. He took a further step. "You don't have the guts, the strength or the technique."

"My father taught me to shoot from fourteen," she said. "Itchen Valley Shooting Club." Her finger tightened on the trigger.

Bluff or not, the bouncer stopped. He tensed, alert. Blood still crept down his shirt and drops fell to the floor. "You won't last," he said.

Rob detected movement in his peripheral vision and the professor was upon him. The sword swung and he parried, twisted to the side. They faced each other, six feet apart.

"A fair fight this time," Rob said. "Tougher now that we're both armed."

The professor smiled. He looked comfortable and gave a few flourishes of the sword. "You have no idea how to use a sword," he said.

"I've been practising," Rob said, and Marianne rolled her eyes.

The professor attacked and Rob defended. Breaking through the professor's defences might be beyond him, but his powers gave him the reactions to anticipate strikes. Constant motion, concentration and fast reactions kept the professor at bay.

They circled round the room, Rob sidestepping or dodging blows, or blocking them with his sword. After sixty seconds—which seemed a long time—Rob found himself close to Kate. He held up an arm. "One moment," he said. The professor was thrown for a second—enough for Rob to twist back and tap his sword on Kate's gun. "One for all," he said.

Her attention on the bouncer didn't waver, but she said, softly, "All for one."

The professor lunged forward and struck at Rob's left midriff. Rob moved to block, but the sword was no longer there and heading for his opposite side. He managed to leap back and deflect the remnant of the blow. He gained confidence and started throwing in some of the moves he'd learnt. He performed short advances and retreats. Threw in feints and strikes, attempted an offensive riposte after blocking one strike. Even managed a lunge. Lots of blocks, but his best defensive technique was simply to move away. The ring of steel echoed round the chamber, and they covered all corners, darting and leaping, advancing and swerving and retreating.

The rest of them remained frozen in their positions. Kate and the bouncer engaged in their staring competition. Paul and Marianne watched intently and shouted words of warning or encouragement.

Rob was too much on the defensive, the onslaught relentless. The professor pushed him towards the middle of the room and he changed things. A rapid leap back, then an acceleration forward and up and he flew at the side wall. The flying still felt fragile but it worked and he kicked off the wall and aimed behind the professor, struck at him before landing. The professor just managed to turn and block, and Rob followed up. The professor blocked again and retreated. He stopped and rested a moment. "You learn quickly," he said.

"You can't achieve anything here," Rob said. "You have no end game."

"On the contrary. You've caused me enormous problems. I'll take immense satisfaction in crushing you. Beyond that, I have contingencies. I'll take the sample I need from Marianne. I need to reboot my operation but my aims will be achieved—just a little later than planned."

The bouncer spoke. No sign of weakness showed in his voice, but blood matted his shirt. "Professor Wolf. Our plan is unchanged. Disarm him and we'll take the gun." The professor ignored him and raised his sword again.

Rob assessed the situation. Kate still held the gun with rigid concentration, but her face was white and she bit her lip. Marianne flexed at her bonds to no result and showed frustration. Paul worked his knots from his awkward, prone position—progress was slow, if at all. Rob prepared to block the professor again, not sure he could win. Then he saw. A tension in the calf, the tiniest of muscle flexes. Jerome was conscious.

Rob blocked the next strike with renewed hope. He thought he heard further noise in the walkway. He couldn't concentrate on it, though, as the professor advanced with increased aggression. In the event, he only had ten seconds to hold out.

A loud bang sounded on the entrance door and a firm voice

rang through, "Police. We're coming in."

The professor lunged towards Rob. He executed a series of strikes and thrusts, and a final sideways swipe—which Rob only just dodged—and leapt past. He took the steps down to the exit door in one stride, yanked it open and departed.

Rob saw the other door opening, took a breath…and followed the professor.

*****

These stairs were much narrower. Hard to pass anyone, never mind swing a sword. He had the choice of up or down. The clatter of sword against the walls gave away the professor's upward direction. Rob sprinted after him, bouncing off the walls as the steps spiralled. Darkness dominated but thin slits in the walls admitted scraps of light from outside, and his eyes adjusted enough to see shapes and outlines. He raced past a narrow door to the bell room on the left, about forty steps up. His legs struggled and he breathed heavily. This wasn't the overwhelming fatigue of earlier. It was a normal fatigue. He ran at the speed of a fit and determined person, unable to surge to superhuman effort. Another fifty steps, and he rounded a curve in the wall and jammed to a halt. The professor faced him in the gloom, sword pointing. The door to the roof lay just beyond.

They both recovered breath a moment.

"Were you going to shoot us?" Rob said.

A hesitation and then the professor said, "For me to know." Another pause and he added, "You've done me a favour. My clients had become too controlling." He pushed his sword forward, idly threatening.

Rob backed off a step. "Much good it'll do you."

The professor made a more menacing jab of the sword. "Advantages and disadvantages. I consider this a draw."

"Really. There's nowhere to go."

The professor lunged at high speed and executed a series of thrusts and short swings. Rob couldn't hold him. He retreated and lost balance, falling backwards and landing on his side.

The professor pushed the door open. "By the way," he said. "Not a bad guess about the crown jewels." He disappeared through the door, with a final "Give my regards to Marianne." The door slammed behind him.

Rob pulled himself to his feet. He approached the door and found it wedged shut. He pushed to no effect, then regathered himself and used what seemed the last vestiges of superpower to barge through.

He ventured onto the rooftop: the summit of a squat Norman tower, about fifteen metres square. The perimeter was defined by a stone wall, two foot high. The centre section had railings around a raised and vented metal structure, designed to allow the sound of the bells to escape. A sword had been casually abandoned on top. To the west and twelve metres below, the ridge of the nave roof stretched away. Patches of ground were visible, forty-five metres down. There was no reasonable way off. And no sign of the professor.

He was captured for a moment. The view provided true splendour here. Glorious in daylight, but a different kind of beauty now: city lights randomly sprinkled across the landscape; the shadows of St Catherine's Hill and St Giles Hill; old churches poking through the buildings; much of the cultural heritage he'd spent last year visiting, if you knew where to look…. He spun towards the door, no time for this now.

*****

Rob sped down the stairs. He ran into Paul halfway, who squeezed against the wall to let him pass. He burst into the ringing chamber. A uniformed policewoman attended to Kate. She sat against the wall and a proper bandage had been applied. She still looked white, but almost laughed when she saw him and Rob was touched.

"How are you…how is she?" Rob asked, addressing both.

Kate didn't speak but reached her hand out and gave a thumbs-up signal. Rob mirrored her and they touched knuckles. The policewoman said, "She'll be all right. There's a squad car outside and we're about to take her to hospital."

The bouncer sat in a chair on the opposite side of the room, handcuffed behind his back. A policeman guarded him. His shirt had been undone and a rudimentary clean-up performed. Deep scratches could be seen.

A man stood in the middle of the room and, accompanied by firm gestures, spoke clear commands into a radio. He was mid-forties, with short, dark hair, about five foot nine, and wore jeans and leather jacket. His air of control was tempered by wary glances at an anteater standing nearby.

He jerked his head in Rob's direction. "Where's Professor Wolf?" he said.

"He's…gone. I'm not sure how."

"We'll search the grounds." He returned to the radio.

Marianne approached. She shrugged, appeared…wary? bashful? "That's Detective Inspector O'Neill," she said. "And well done."

Rob checked the room again. "Where's Jerome?"

"I don't know. The police were trying to restrain the professor's accomplice—he's a known and dangerous criminal, by the way—and somewhere in the confusion he vanished."

Paul appeared from the stairway. He joined them and shook Rob's hand. "Good routine," he said.

Rob clapped him on the back. "Fantastic," he said. Neither of them could keep from smiling.

"You guys practised that?" Marianne said.

"Sort of—" Rob said.

"Without the smoke bombs," Paul said.

The policewoman started to lead Kate from the room and back along the walkway. Marianne volunteered to go with her, but the Inspector called her back. "I'd like to talk to you, please," he said. He shifted his gaze to Rob. "I definitely want to talk to you." Paul went with Kate. Rob and Marianne wished her luck, said they'd be along later.

The Inspector asked if they should contact anyone for Kate. Rob mentioned Arnold. Marianne rolled her eyes for about the fifth time that day. The Inspector made a call, passed on the information. A voice came over the radio and he answered, spoke a while, ending with, "Yes, the zoo. I don't care what time it is, wake them up. I'm on my second shift myself."

He turned to face them, glancing at Hector on the way. He raised his eyes to the ceiling and breathed deeply. He addressed Marianne first. "Ms Golding, I understand you've been through an ordeal, but I need to ask you about your links with Professor Mark Wolf. Through our prisoner here"—he nodded at the bouncer—"he's connected with a very serious group of people. We've been monitoring the relationship, but we don't understand the connection."

"He asked me to help on a project," she said. "Inflammatory disease mechanisms. Over time, he started acting strange and controlling. He terminated my project and I'm sure he stole some of my work from my house last week. Next time I saw him, I was tied up here. I can write up the details."

"Did you report the theft?"

"I'm sorry, Inspector. I haven't had time."

"Ok. I will need that statement."

Marianne nodded.

The Inspector turned to Rob. "You're Rob Griffin?"

"Yes."

"We have one excellent result, Mr Griffin. We've needed evidence against our friend on the chair and his associates for a long time. After tonight's episode I can obtain warrants and tear through the whole organisation."

"I'm glad we could help," Rob said.

"I'm also puzzled. We received two calls tonight. One from a student in Wales and one from a local resident about an illegally parked car—yours, in fact. The student mentioned Professor Wolf, which is why I was woken. His name is linked to my investigation, although he hasn't committed any crime I'm aware of. Until tonight, anyway."

The anteater walked past them and stopped at the front of the room.

"What's the puzzle?" Rob said.

The Inspector ticked items off on his fingers. "I have two reports of a man flying in the Badger Farm area. A car similar to yours was reported on the A3090, where a man was seen bundling a struggling figure inside. Your car, which is now parked outside, contains a stolen painting. Two people were kidnapped and tied up. A respected professor has shot and injured your friend—who quite superbly held off a dangerous criminal. Jerome Laroche, a suspect in the Velvet Vandal case my colleague is investigating, was here when we arrived but has now disappeared. There's obviously been a sword fight. And an anteater is wandering about the room." He fixed Rob with a stare. "I presume you can explain all this?"

"Er…yes. Can I do a statement like Marianne?"

"Nine o'clock in the morning, as soon as the station opens."

Rob remembered something, pulled out his phone and showed the Inspector a picture. "This is where the Round Table is," he said.

The Inspector looked at it, lightened up, even came close to a smile. "We would never have found that." Rob closed his eyes a moment, tired, and the Inspector paused. "I tell you what. Someone will give you a call round about noon, but you can do the statement Monday."

Two police came to help escort the prisoner away and a dog handler to try and manage the anteater. Rob gave Hector a friendly salute, and Rob and Marianne left. They traversed the walkway—well-lit now—and descended the stairs to the Cathedral nave. Rob diverted to Jane Austen's ledgerstone in the north aisle. The memorial plaque had been restored to the wall. He smiled, and joined Marianne at the exit. They emerged into a dark and deserted Cathedral Close at one in the morning.

Rob called Paul. Kate was fine, but sedated and asleep. Best to visit after a night's sleep. Paul reminded him of the tennis final, which started at two in the afternoon, and that he needed to recuperate.

Rob's car was still there, alongside a couple of police cars. Presumably the gates had been opened, and Rob offered Marianne a lift. He halted a moment and said, "My powers have been waxing and waning all day. They're good for a while, then I get fatigued and they're gone. After the fight tonight, it's like they're completely drained." He glanced into her eyes, then away. "They will be back tomorrow, won't they?"

She didn't answer.

Rob leaned on the car. The elm where he and Paul had rescued the cat was off to the left. Events from the year flickered through his mind: Marianne's secret cellar, meeting Kate at the clinic, discovering his powers at North Walls Recreation Ground, unveiling his detective agency, flying above Old Winchester Hill with Kate, the battle with the Velvet Vandal on the Westgate, the trip to Oxford with Paul…right up to tonight's adventure. "There are so many things left to do," he said. A faint smile. "And the flying is unbelievable."

She put a hand on his shoulder. "I'm sorry, Rob."

Epilogue

Rebecca recognised the handwriting. She opened the envelope. Inside was a typewritten report and a personal letter addressed to her. She read the letter. Smiled, even blushed a little. She scanned the report before taking it to the editor's office.

The editor read it through.

"His final report," Rebecca said. "Can we run it?"

"Well, technically he is a fugitive," the editor said.

"But he's one of ours. And we've just got time to make tomorrow's edition."

The editor smiled. "Hold the front page," she said.

Hampshire Cup provides exciting climax
by Jerome Laroche

Once again I am here to tell you a striking tale. Something different this time. I shall become a sports reporter and hope you can be satisfied. But there is more that I shall weave into my narrative. For reasons you may be appraised of, I will be leaving town a while. The end of a summer of adventure is here and the Velvet Vandal has run his last mission. I hope you will not be shocked at my own involvement, but I give a small defence. Not only has the Velvet Vandal placed culture to the fore of our minds—the priceless artefacts from time long-disappeared, the echoes of ancient history and battles, the skill of artists and performers— but a whole new story is built with heroes, villains, romance and adventure. Perhaps that is enough.

Now for the tennis. The protagonists are Roger

Shepard, champion in five of the last seven years, and Rob Griffin, surprise first-time finalist. I am at the back of the stands wearing dark glasses and a wide-brimmed hat. A man and a well-behaved dog—a collie—are next to me. Roger wins the first two games and it is apparent Rob is struggling. He is slow to the ball, but more than that. One point will demonstrate. The shots are deep and the rally is good, eight...ten...twelve shots. Roger pushes the ball wide to the forehand side and Rob hits back and moves to the centre for the next shot. Roger hits another to the forehand and Rob runs to hit back and now Roger goes wide to the backhand and Rob sprints but can't reach it. He is surprised. His body is not doing what he expects and he shakes his head. The set continues in this vein. Rob runs for everything and wins a game, but he looks tired and Roger takes the first set 6-1.

Rob speaks to his coach before the second set. Here I will divert and introduce the coach. His name is Paul Martin. Next to him is a naturally chic lady. She wears a scarf, casually draped, and large sunglasses, an elegant jacket and skirt. She could be French, though I know she is not. A young boy is to her side playing with his phone. Now the payoff. This morning Paul has become engaged to the lady, Sarah. I have inside information and the occasion was a country drive and a walk to their favourite spot, on Beacon Hill, high on the Downs near Warnford. Rob and Paul confer. Rob listens as Paul explains tactics. He makes practice shots and moves but appears downcast. A lady enters the arena. You notice her arm is in a sling, but that is not the main thing to notice. She is tall and blonde and slim, mid-thirties perhaps but looks younger, casual in jeans and.... Enough, this is a tennis report. The front sections are full and she sits in the opposite stand to me. She waves to Rob and he sees her and smiles. I think she recognises me and she waves to me, also. I hold a hand up but keep my head down, try to avoid the attention.

Before you think I am a bad sports reporter, like a dog chasing many different stories, let me tell you the second set has started. Rob serves the first game and changes to his game are apparent. He knows he needs to hit the ball deep or there is no chance, and he executes this well, most shots to Roger's backhand. He runs a little less and anticipates a little better. He still chases all over the court to near the limit but gives up on some unreachable shots, preserves some energy. The real change is something else. He takes more risks. He is winning the first game 40-30 and we are ten shots into the rally. This is the point that matters and his concentration is turned to maximum. Roger hits a three-quarters length ball and Rob gambles and attacks. A hard shot to the backhand and a dart to the net. Roger lobs but Rob can reach it and smashes, the ball nudging the sideline. Rob is 1-0 up. They stay in step and win their service games until 3-3. Roger wins his games more easily. He can serve and volley, and effortlessly find angles, but Rob scrambles his games. The next game, Roger breaks to lead 4-3. Rob is too attacking and is picked off at the net. Roger holds serve and is 5-3 up. Rob grits his teeth and holds serve but Roger is serving for the match at 5-4.

Rob goes for broke and it works. He hammers shots to the lines and goes 0-30 up. Roger pulls back to 30-30, but follows with a double fault, his second serve missing by an inch. Rob runs over the whole court on the next point and can hardly move at the end, but Roger hits the tape on shot twenty and the score's back to 5-5. They swap games and it's 6-6 with a tie-break to come. Roger suddenly seems human—tired and feeling pressure. Tennis is easier when you're winning. When the game is close, every point and decision matters and pressure builds—the key is to build a lead and relax, enjoy the game. The tie-break stays close and there is no relaxing. The players appear equal. The score is 1-1, then 2-2, 3-3, 4-4, 5-5. Rob hits a return in the corner to force an error for 6-5 and a set point. A rally progresses and Roger comes to the net on shot eight. The ball was short but only a little and he takes a risk. Rob aims for the pass and he bends his knee, winds his arm back. This for the set. He hits it well and Roger is beaten at the net. The ball arrows toward the baseline. But no. Inches long. Back to six points all. Roger wins the next two points and takes the match 6-1 7-6 and the Hampshire Cup for the sixth time.

Rob stares at the floor. For an instant he had a chance. He looks up to sustained applause for both players. He has made a magnificent effort against a top player and I think he realises this. He applauds Roger, raises an arm, and turns in a circle so all the spectators see him. Roger meets him at the net, claps him on the shoulder and shakes his hand for several seconds. He must have been worried, but we congratulate Roger on adding to his tremendous record. His mum is watching and he speaks to her. A modest wave to the crowd.

As we wait for the presentation, there is another lady I haven't mentioned. Slim and dark-haired, brown eyes, freckles. Intense and driven but with a playful side. I could continue, but hang on, you say. Anyway, she speaks to Roger. He appears wary but then they are laughing and she hugs him. She stops in front of Rob and Rob bows. They talk and are comfortable, and she hugs him also. I am missing out. Then she is gone, a quick chat with the lady with the sling on the way out. I try to find her after the match. I see her in the distance, but then—you will scarce believe this—she accelerates across the ground and flies away. Somewhere towards Eastleigh. Her office tells me she's resigned to "help the world". I must search for this lady as a matter of high seriousness. She has a powerful destiny and my intentions are honourable.

Back to the match. It is finished, but the presentation is to come. Rob takes the runner-up trophy. He is wistful but proud, I think. Roger raises the Hampshire Cup. Photos are taken, and talk and laughter is on court, and the crowd start to leave. The lady with the sling makes her way to the front and talks to Rob. Much activity is around them, and they blend into the background and stumble on a little privacy. She says something and Rob gives a modest shrug, and Rob says something and she laughs, and she touches his arm, and Rob stops, like a spaceship has landed, and looks at her. Rob leans forward, and so does she, and then, amongst the organisers clearing the courtside, and the crowd packing and leaving, and Roger giving a final, small wave and walking his mum towards the exit, and Paul and Sarah sharing some strawberries they have brought, and the young boy kicking a tennis ball about court like he is David Beckham, they kiss. For a long time. They look into eyes and say a few words, and then a shorter kiss, a touch of the lips. Paul sees them, and they look up and see him, and he raises a hand, smiles. Sarah and the young boy say farewell and depart with the last of the crowd. Rob, Paul and the lady linger a while before leaving together. I think they go to the pub.

This is my match report and perhaps my only go at sports reporting. As promised, other tales are amongst the points. Some of these may seem disconnected, but they are personal to me and you will excuse my indulgence. I add another, not reported elsewhere. Mark Wolf, Oxford Professor of Biochemistry and international figure, has disappeared—last seen in Winchester and leaving behind a mystery lab and some shady connections. A moment, though. I reveal my tales are not so random—I am a professional, after all—but are linked to the story of the summer, the Velvet Vandal. This is not the worldwide story I hoped, but stories are unpredictable and cannot be controlled.

Here is the important thing. Somewhere, Rob, Paul, the lady with the sling, the lady who helps the world, and the rest—myself, even—are out there, living our stories. I mention also Culture Man, whose identity I choose not to reveal, and wonder if he'll reappear. Anyway, they are having successes and setbacks, trying to find purpose and build careers, looking for love. The same we all do, and these stories are important. For these characters, a little more though. Once the taste of adventure is within you, once you have battled villains, once you have flown the skies, once you have rescued cats and created superpower potions and been a physio to superheroes and infiltrated enemy labs, once you have experienced cathedral-top showdowns, then the call stays with you. What I try to say is that there will be more feats and escapades to tell and I will return. Be aware that I will keep you informed.

END

About the Author and Author Notes

About the Author

I was born and grew up in the county of Somerset, England. After a degree in mathematical physics, I've moved through a number of jobs including seismic exploration, software programming, project management and bid management. Residing in Winchester for the last ten years, I seem to have settled here—the culture is top rate. I play tennis and climb the odd mountain. I can't fly or run the hundred metres in six seconds.

Story Notes

Culture Man is my first book-length story and I hope you've enjoyed it. The Year of Culture actually happened, in 2009, and the blog entries are adapted from my own blog. Despite this, Culture Man is absolutely, definitely, not me.

Previous Stories, Future Stories and Sporting Tales

I've published one previous short story, The Overarm Dog, which is a tale of action, suspense, romance…and a dog learning the front crawl. The link between the stories is sports fiction, although the sport only provides a loose backdrop—like any story, they're about human dreams, actions and challenges. As such, I've set up the Sporting Tales Facebook page and website. The Facebook page will keep you up to date with day to day activities and new projects, and let you post and interact. The website gives a summary.

www.facebook.com/sportingtales

www.sportingtales.co.uk

Reviews

Any online reviews are much appreciated ☺. Please go to the Amazon page and scroll down to find the "Write a customer review" button.

Culture Man's Winchester

(not to scale)

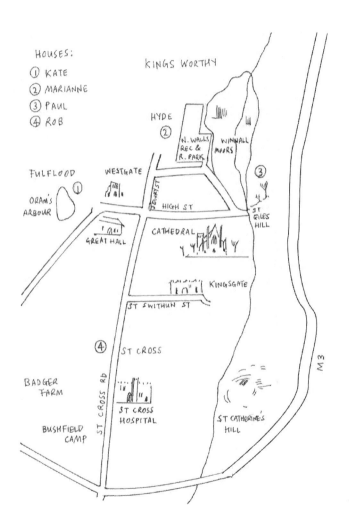

HOUSES:
① KATE
② MARIANNE
③ PAUL
④ ROB

Printed in Poland
by Amazon Fulfillment
Poland Sp. z o.o., Wrocław